Double Dutch Death
Bells and Blazes

The Frannie Shoemaker Campground Series

Bats and Bones
The Blue Coyote
Peete and Repeat
The Lady of the Lake
To Cache a Killer
A Campy Christmas
The Space Invader
Real Actors, Not People
Corpse of Discovery
Mask of Death
We Are NOT Buying a Camper! (prequel)

Also by Karen Musser Nortman

The Time Travel Trailer
Trailer on the Fly
Trailer, Get Your Kicks!
Happy Camper Tips and Recipes

Dedicated to the Midwest Glampers

Siblings

and

Sneakiness

The Mystery Sisters Book 5

by Karen Musser Nortman

Cover Art by Ace Book Covers

TABLE OF CONTENTS

CHAPTER ONE

"I STILL THINK this is a bad idea," Maxine Berra said. "We could have easily gotten a hotel and just come out here during the day for visits."

"It would have been expensive, and you're the one who never wants to spend money," her sister Lil answered.

Max's red Studebaker crept along the campground road. Trees heavy with the emerald leaves of late summer and some with golds and reds of early fall arched overhead, filtering the afternoon sunlight. A few stately pines poked their spires among the blaze of color. Lil hung her head out the passenger window gawking, while Max's Irish Setter, Rosie, did the same thing from the back seat. Although it was more likely that Rosie was watching for squirrels, rather than the quaint little abodes tucked in the trees that Lil was gushing over.

"Oh, look at that one! It looks like a gypsy trailer!" Lil pointed at a small, rounded camper that was painted dark red with a stripe around the middle that looked like gold lace. A canopy over the front appeared to be a silky material in jewel-toned stripes and edged in gold fringe.

1

Max kept her eyes on the twists and turns on the road. "Yeah, yeah, yeah. What campsite did Carole say she would be in?"

"Number 21, I think." The car rounded a curve and Lil pointed again. "And that one's done with a cowboy theme—I can't wait to see inside these."

"Blah, blah. Watch for 21. That was 27 so we must be getting close."

"She said her trailer is red and white. Oh, I see her!" Lil pointed ahead and Rosie barked.

Max frowned. "That camper is tiny. I knew we should have gotten a hotel." She pulled her classic car into a gravel pad alongside a red pickup. "At least we're color coordinated."

"Stop your grumbling." Lil opened her door to greet their sister.

A short woman hurried toward their car, smiling and clapping her hands. Carole was their youngest sister and resembled Lil more than Max. Max was tall, somewhat athletic-looking, and disdained makeup and salons as a waste of time. She wore her salt-and-pepper hair in a short, low-maintenance bob. Lil and Carole both had soft blond curls framing their faces and loved an afternoon in a beauty or makeup salon.

Carole leaned in the open door and hugged Lil. "I'm so glad you made it! I've enjoyed this group so much, and I thought 'What could be a more fun weekend than to share it with my sisters?'" Max rolled her eyes at Lil. Carole noticed and babbled on. "Don't give us that

2

look. Did you have any problems? I can't wait to show you everything. I've got some glasses of iced tea on the table, and we'll unload your stuff later."

Max opened the door and unfolded herself from the low seat, grunting a little. Carole came around and gave her a hug too. "No problems at all—a nice drive," Max said. "I'll let Rosie stretch her legs and then join you. Nothing stronger than iced tea?"

Carole laughed. "Same old Max. Later. Tea for now." Max reached back and grabbed a leash before releasing Rosie from the back seat. Although Rosie wasn't young, Max was long past catching her if she got away.

As Max headed down the campground road, pulled by the setter, Carole guided Lil to the picnic table, her arm around her sister's shoulders.

The retro-looking little trailer, framed by tall, overarching hardwoods, presented a welcoming tableau. A striped awning—red and white, of course—sprouted from the side of the little trailer. The picnic table, centered a short distance from the trailer door, was covered by a red gingham cloth. An old Campbell's soup can crammed with red zinnias took up the center.

Lil turned around taking in the whole campsite before sitting on the bench. "This is awesome! When you said you bought a camper, you didn't tell me that you had it completely decorated and accessorized." She pointed at a vintage red kitchen stool standing by one end of the trailer with an old picnic basket on the seat,

3

and a stack of red Samsonite suitcases at the other end. "Where did you get all of that stuff?"

Carole giggled. "There's not much left in the local thrift shops." Then she sobered. "It's something to do—take my mind off—you know." Tears filled her eyes.

Lil drew her into a hug. "Oh, honey, I'm *so* sorry I haven't gotten back here since the funeral. I *know* what a void you are feeling, losing Bob, and should have been here for you."

Carole sniffed and pulled back. "Don't be silly. I should have been there for *you*. How awful that you had to go through that knee replacement twice."

"Don't fret—Max was there."

Carole wiped her tears and grinned. "That's what I mean. I should have been there. Our sister is not known for her bedside manner."

Lil grimaced. "Or her cooking." She glanced around to make sure Max hadn't returned. "Thank goodness for carry-out."

Carole patted Lil's hand. "Well, speaking of your knee, let's find you a comfortable seat. How about this chair? I can find you something for a footstool."

"Just a regular chair will be fine. If I need something else, I'll tell you. So how are you really doing? Did you get Bob's estate all settled?"

"Yeah, that wasn't too bad." Carole sighed. "Everything, though, triggers a memory. *You* know. I get out a couple of new lawn chairs at home that we picked out last year when we thought we would have years together. Songs we danced to, a dust rag that's one of his old shirts, a Santa Fe brochure in the desk for a trip we were thinking about. I'm sure you went through that too."

Lil nodded. "I still find things of Earl's that choke me up. And he's been gone five years."

"So none of this" — Carole waved her hand around the site, — "has any memories of Bob connected to it. But, besides missing him, I don't feel I know my place any more in our circle of friends. I'm not a fifth wheel, I'm a half wheel. You know, you've been there too — it's a couples' society."

She paused and looked off in to the woods. "I have friends at home who are also widowed, and we do things together, but I feel sort of cut off from all of our old friends. I mean, they're still friends, but I'm not in those social circles any more. That's how I got involved with this group," — she indicated the campers lining the road with a wave of her hand, — "my friend Lois lost her husband three years ago. They had always been big campers, and she didn't want to quit. So she sold their fifth wheel and bought that blue and white Shasta across the road and joined this group — the Galloping Glampers."

Max and Rosie returned. "What have I missed?"

Carole looked up and smiled. "Sit. I was just telling Lil how I got into this group." She told Max about Lois, and they all looked toward the little blue and white trailer. "That's an old one," Carole said. "Lois actually rebuilt a lot of it herself and it's great. She invited me to go with her on a weekend gathering and I was hooked. Mine is a reproduction, but I've had so much fun furnishing it."

Max looked around at the variety of campers, mostly small and many vintage. "So all of these women are widows?" She took a seat at the table.

"Oh, no! Some of the group are divorced, some have husbands who come with them, and some of their husbands just don't like to camp or can't because of jobs. Anyway, I feel very comfortable in this group and they do such fun things. And I'm *so* excited to have you share it."

"Is everyone in the campground part of your group?" Max asked.

"No—just these eight or ten sites on both sides of the road here. Down around that curve, there are other campers. Look past those maples there—you can just see the front of a big motorhome. They aren't part of our group."

Lil sat forward in her chair and clasped her hands. "What's on the agenda for this weekend?"

"Well," Carole said, "about 5:00 this evening, four of the women are going to do a taco bar, and the rest of us will bring appetizers and dessert. After supper, we'll have a campfire and initiate a new member. Tomorrow morning, we're going to tour the round barn. Did you notice that as you came in? Near the entrance to the park?"

"Yes," Max said. "It looks interesting."

"It's supposed to be. One of the few left in the state. Then after lunch, Becky is going to teach us how to make woven place mats. Later her husband is going to talk about repacking wheel bearings."

"*That* sounds exciting," Max said dryly.

Carole shrugged. "Probably not, but the old trailers require that. On Sunday morning, we're going to hike to a waterfall that's in the park. We'll see if you are up to that, Lil. We don't have to do it. But right now, before supper, I thought we'd take a little tour of some of the campers."

"Goody!" Lil said, which made Max raise her eyebrows.

"Are you seven?"

Lil stuck out her tongue. "Yes. At heart. Better than being an old dried-up stick-in-the-mud." She grinned. "Let's start with yours, Carole, and then we can unload our things. There's room for all of us in there?" She looked at the little trailer with some misgivings.

"It will be cozy, but it will work," Carole said. "Come on."

Max looked skeptical, but tied Rosie's leash to the leg of the picnic table. Carole held the door for them. Inside, a black and white checked floor caught the eye first. To the right of the entrance, around the front end, was a dinette booth with red leatherette seats. Small windows surrounding that area were dressed with tie-back curtains made from dishtowels with red stripes. Overhead cupboards topped the windows.

On the wall facing the door, a short run of light wood cupboards held a small sink and a three-burner gas stove. Two red metal canisters stood on the counter. A red kit-cat clock with a swinging tail hung on the wall above the counter, next to two red and black hot pads. The ticking sound added a comfortable ambience. A small couch, also in red leatherette, filled the other end next to a door.

"The dinette makes into a bed where two of us can sleep, and the other person gets the couch," Carole said. She opened the door beside the couch. "Behold, the bathroom!"

Max peered around the door. "There's a shower, but no curtain or stall."

Carole laughed. "It's called a wet bath. The whole space is the shower stall. But there's a shower house a few sites down and we'll probably all use that."

Max humphed. "Okayyy."

"I emptied one of the overhead cupboards by the dinette for each of you. You can put your things in there."

"Mine will fit," Max said, "but Lil, you might have to leave *one* of your suitcases in the car."

Lil didn't rise to the bait. "That's fine. I'll just shift some things around."

It took much jostling and do-si-do-ing for the two women to get their belongings crammed in the overhead cupboards. Carole sat out under the awning, knowing

8

from experience it was best for her to stay out of her older sisters's way. She could hear Max's strident complaints with Lil trying to shush her. When they emerged, their surly faces were enough to make her comment brightly, "Well, did that work?"

Lil smiled. "Yes, it's fine. So, now can we see some of these others?"

Carole got up. "Sure thing. We'll see who's home." She turned to Max. "What about Rosie?"

"She'll be fine for a bit."

When they started up the road, Lil said, "I especially want to see that gypsy one."

Carole frowned. "Which one is the gypsy one?"

"Oh, that's just what it makes me think of. The dark red one." Lil pointed up the road.

"That's Becky's, and I see her out there now. We'll start there."

Max had no expectations. In her mind, this seemed like a lot of work for a couple of days of so-called fun. She suspected that once a woman invested in one of these campers, she felt a commitment to carry on whether she liked it or not. Maybe not, but surely everyone wasn't as enthusiastic as Carole.

They walked up the road, and Carole called out "Becky! Someone here to meet you!"

Becky looked up from the box of firewood that she was unloading near the campfire and pushed a lock of brown hair away from her round, flushed face. She grinned and wiped her hands on her jeans as she came forward.

"Becky, these are my sisters — *much* older sisters, I might add — and they're going to be spending the weekend with us. This is Lil from Kansas and Max from Colorado. And they especially want to see your camper. Lil called it a 'gypsy camper.'"

Becky held out her hand and shook with both of them. "Great to meet you. Lil, is it? and Max. Welcome to the Galloping Glampers." She looked back at her trailer. "Gypsy, huh? I guess it does have that look, and I have no problem with that. Let me give you the tour."

Max thought 'tour' may have been too generous a term since it implied distance and roaming through various rooms. Checking out a fourteen or sixteen foot camper required more of a side-step shuffle dance and not much time. Paisley and other Eastern-looking print fabrics were draped to cover the walls. Two woven ribbon place mats in jewel-bright tones flanked a brass candle-holder on the little dinette.

"I love everything you've done," Lil said. "It's *so* exotic!"

Max agreed. "Very unique and not at all what I expected."

Carole pointed at the table. "Those are the place mats that Becky is going to teach us to make. Her husband Greg is the one who's going to tell us all about wheel bearings."

"Your husband camps with you?" Max asked. "He doesn't mind the decor?"

10

Becky laughed. "We have another camper — a fifth wheel that we use when we camp on our own or take longer trips. But he's a good sport about this and tolerates the close quarters for a couple of days. He enjoys this group."

Carole nodded. "He's a good guy, and a great help for things that are out of our wheelhouse. Thanks, Becky."

They headed out the door. The next trailer was larger and decorated in a Western theme. Large, forties-style decals of lasso-wielding cowgirls in short skirts and cowboy hats decorated the exterior. The owner, Patrice, a petite fortyish woman in fitted jeans and a blue-checked shirt that complimented her rich dark skin, greeted them warmly and ushered them into her restored Argosy.

"This is bigger than most of the ones here," Max commented. "How long is it?"

"Twenty-six feet," Patrice said. She pointed out the twin beds in the back covered with denim bedspreads and the comfortable couch across the front under a big window. Red bandana fabric curtained the windows, and rope edged the countertop.

"Wonderful!" Lil said. "Do you get out in it much?"

Patrice nodded and smiled. "In the summer. I teach so I don't get much time during the school year. But I never miss a Galloping Glamper outing!"

As they left Patrice's site, Max said, "I must admit, I'm pleasantly surprised. I expected that they would all be full of lace and Victorian froufrou."

Carole laughed. "Well, this next one is. Not Victorian, but plenty of froufrou."

They crossed the road to a pink and white Scotty. Carole tapped on the door and it was opened by a tall woman with dark hair cut in a pixie.

"Hi, Carole. Are these your guests?"

Carole introduced Max and Lil to Leah Groton. Max was overwhelmed by Barbie pink throughout the interior. She was reminded of the line from the movie *Steel Magnolias*—something about the church looking like a bottle of Pepto Bismol had exploded. The dinette table, flanked by benches upholstered in pink checked fabric, was covered with a lace tablecloth and lit by a crystal chandelier. A pink princess phone sat on a ledge above the dinette, along with a pink toaster.

"Wow!" Lil pointed at the phone. "Does that work?"

"Oh, it works," Leah said, "But it's not hooked up. It's just for show."

"Isn't that chandelier amazing?" Carole said. "She made it from her mother's old jewelry."

Max nodded. "That's an excellent job." Lil elbowed Carole and grinned.

Leah waved a hand. "I had help from You Tube. And it wasn't just my mother's jewelry. I found pieces in thrift shops on some of our Glamper weekends."

"I love thrift shops," Lil said, "but Max doesn't have much patience with them."

Leah looked envious. "But it's so great that you can travel together. You must have a wonderful relationship."

Max snorted. "What do you think, Lil? Do we have a wonderful relationship?"

"They argue *all* of the time," Carole said with a grin.

Lil looked embarrassed. "Yes, we do argue a lot, but if we didn't have a good relationship, we wouldn't be able to do this at all."

Leah said, "You're right. My sister hasn't spoken to me in years. Ever since our mother died. She is convinced that I got more than she did—that Mom settled a large chunk of money on me before she died that never went through the estate. It's ridiculous—most of Mother's money went to pay for her care in the nursing home. But Tammy is convinced that somehow I got more than she did, and she cut herself off completely. So I envy you."

Max put one arm around Lil's shoulders and the other around Carole. "She's right. We are lucky."

Carole bent over and looked past Max to Lil. "Aliens," she said in a stage whisper. "Aliens have taken our sister."

CHAPTER TWO

AS THEY LEFT Leah's trailer, and headed to her camper, Carole said, "We have about an hour until supper. Do you want to look at any more?"

"Let's just walk down to the end of the campground and check out how the other half lives," Lil said. "I could use a little more walking. Too much time in the car today."

Carole laughed. "I could *always* use that!"

Once they passed the last of the Glampers' sites and rounded the curve, a wide variety of temporary abodes greeted them. Supper preparations were underway at most sites, children raced up and down the road on bikes and skateboards, and people called back and forth to friends.

"It almost looks like they're preparing for the D-Day invasion," Max said.

"I don't think the soldiers were this happy about that project," Lil said.

"I suppose not."

Carole nodded toward a setup that they were passing. "I guess here's what you do when you have a lot of kids."

A 'pop up,' a tent perched on a trailer with enclosed beds sprouting out the front and the back, took up the center of the gravel area. Two small tents—one red and yellow and the other blue decorated with superheroes, flanked the picnic table. An eight or nine-year old boy chased his younger sister with a squirt gun, while two older boys hunched in lawn chairs, thumbs flying over their video games.

A youngish woman in a tee shirt and gray leggings sat in a chaise lounge with a frosty drink and a paperback. She looked up at the women walking down the road, rolled her eyes in the direction of the kids, and shrugged her shoulders.

"Good luck!" Lil called out. The woman smiled.

"That's why we have children when we're younger and bum knees when we're older," she whispered to her sisters. "Bum knees are much easier to take."

Carole chuckled. "You got that right."

Across the road from the family, a large newish gray and white fifth-wheel loomed over its neighbors. A middle-aged couple sat in elaborate reclining lawn chairs and appeared to be in a serious discussion, bordering on anger. Max noticed a 'For Sale' sign in a window of the RV. The woman set her beer down hard and stomped up the steps into the camper, slamming the door behind her. The man noticed them and gave them a curt nod.

"Apparently, *all's* not well in Mudville," Max commented.

They reached a turn-around at the end of the road after passing a variety of other units.

"I have a bottle of bourbon in my car, and I think it's past cocktail hour," Max said.

"Yes," Lil agreed. "Let's do some catching up."

Rosie greeted them as if they had been gone for a month. Carole brought some glasses and a bucket of ice out of her camper while Max got her bottle of bourbon from the trunk of her car. Lil produced a bottle of Seven-Up for her bourbon and seven, while Max did the bartender honors. Carole went back in the camper for a plate of cheese and crackers.

They sat in the shade of the awning and sipped their drinks in silence for a few minutes, absorbing the peace of the sun-dappled woods behind the campsite. Fall color peeked from many branches and a cool breeze rustled the leaves.

A tapping sound drew Max's eyes up. She pointed at a high branch on a tall ash tree on the edge of the woods. "I think that's a pileated woodpecker."

"I think you're right," Carole said. "I have some binoculars and a bird book in the camper. I should get them out."

Their attention was diverted from the woods by the sound of slow footsteps on the road. A short, stocky woman with gray-brown curls, trudged up the road. A too-tight red tee shirt and denim capris revealed every extra pound. Her slow pace and slumped shoulders gave her a very dejected look.

"Hi, Babs!" Carole called out.

The woman straightened up, spotted them, and waved. A broad smile removed all trace of the dejection of a moment before.

"Hi, Carole! Are you going to the taco supper?"

"We are. You?"

"You bet! See you there. I'm going to help set up." With that, she continued up the road, maintaining her upbeat stature.

Lil looked at Carole with raised eyebrows. "That was kind of…odd. Do you know her well?"

Carole watched the woman go up the road and used her forefinger and thumb to smooth the crease in her shorts. "I've only been to one other gathering where she was. She's got a sad backstory." She paused and looked up. "Her husband's in prison."

Max snapped her head around and watched Babs. "Really! For what?"

"He had an investment firm and embezzled from some of his clients, including Babs' mother. But most of the time she's pretty upbeat, at least around others. We just caught a glimpse of her when she's not."

Clouds moved across the sun, casting shadows over the campground, and Lil shuddered.

"I guess that just goes to prove that we never really know where someone else lives," Max said.

"What do you mean?" Lil asked.

"That we don't really have a handle on what someone is going through."

17

Carole and Lil raised their eyebrows and looked at each other. It wasn't like their sister to wax philosophical or even show much empathy.

"You're right," Lil said. She turned to Carole. "So do you need to fix something to take to the supper?"

Carole shook her head. "I made brownies. Mother's recipe. And I have ice cream to go with them." She glanced at her watch. "We'll get ready in about fifteen minutes or so. Tell me about your plans. Where's your next trip?"

"Lil wants to go to Texas this winter for a few weeks. I'd like to head for the desert country in the Southwest in time for the spring bloom."

"Couldn't you do both?"

"That's what I said," Lil put in.

Max shrugged. "We could, I guess. Trouble is, we don't have any relatives either place so we'd be looking at a lot of hotel expense."

Carole scoffed. "It's not like either one of you can't afford it."

"How would you know?" Max said, but grinned. "It's none of your beeswax."

"Boy, I haven't heard that in eons," Carole answered.

By the time they visited the restroom, changed shirts, and packed up plates, silverware, brownies, and ice cream, about ten other women, a couple of men and several kids had gathered at an older class C. Unlike the other campers that Carole had shown her sisters, the plain, white-ridged aluminum siding on the exterior hadn't been decorated in any way.

"Whose camper is this?" Lil asked Carole as they approached.

"Her name is Jeanette — Jeanette Walton — but everyone calls her 'Buzzy.' I don't know where that came from. She just bought this camper a couple of months ago and so far has been working on the inside. She's an amazing person. She runs a non-profit for autistic children and adults."

Several picnic tables from adjoining sites had been pulled together and covered with bright-colored cloths. A smaller folding table sported a red, green, and yellow striped tablecloth with slow cookers of meat and bowls of lettuce, tomatoes and cheese arranged on it. Carole put her plate of brownies at the end of the food table with the other desserts and their plates on one of the picnic tables.

"Leah set up a Margarita bar over there," Carole said. "I'll put this ice cream in Buzzy's freezer and then we'll head over there, and I'll introduce you around.

"I won't remember anyone's names," Maxine grumbled.

"No, but they'll remember you."

Lil chuckled. "That's for sure."

"Now, girls, let's not have any fighting," Carole said in a falsetto voice.

"God, you sound just like Mom," Max said, and they turned their attention to the drinks table.

19

Once they had beverages and plates of food, Carole led them toward a half-filled table. On the way, Carole stopped by a full table where a fiftyish woman with brown hair pulled back in a messy bun sat at the end of the bench eating her meal. She wore pink-framed glasses, a Notre Dame sweatshirt, and jeans. "Max and Lil, this is my friend Lois Becker, who got me into this mess."

Lois threw back her head and laughed. "They must be your sisters. I can see the resemblance."

"Now I'm offended," Max said, but smiled. "Seriously, I'm glad to meet you. You have given Carole a new passion, that's for sure."

"Isn't that a great camper? I would have loved to have gotten one of those." Her face clouded for an instant.

"But if I had your skills," Carole said, "I would have gone the route you did. The vintage ones have an ambience that the new ones don't."

Lois shrugged and then brightened. "I think they call that mold, not ambience." She laughed. "Are you going down to the campfire after supper?"

"Definitely," Carole said. "We'll see you there."

They found seats next to Becky, her husband Greg, and Buzzy. Buzzy had long gray hair pulled back in a pony tail at the base of her neck. Excellent bone structure and beautiful skin gave her face a much younger look than her chronological age.

20

Lil said to Buzzy, "What are your plans for your camper? Carole said you haven't had it very long."

Buzzy chewed up a bite of taco and swallowed. "I really don't know yet. Just trying to get the feel of her—you know, read her character."

"Don't believe her," Becky said. "The inside is adorable. Kind of a beach theme. I think she's got the 'feel of her.'"

Greg laughed. "Pretty soon these gals will be hiring psychologists to analyze their campers."

Becky put her hand on Greg's arm. "Max and Lil think my camper has a Gypsy look. Maybe I should learn to read tea leaves and tell fortunes."

"Good idea. Make a little money back to cover your decor. Maybe you could predict whether Amy's baby will be a boy or a girl."

Buzzy looked at Max and Lil. "Becky and Greg are going to become grandparents in a few months. We don't take her shopping with us any more because she can't pass up a baby store."

Becky laughed. "Hey! Just helping the economy."

Buzzy said, "Right. By the way, I had an interesting chat with the campground hostess—"

"Can I sit here?" A thin woman with light brown page boy and dark-rimmed glasses dropped a bag of taco chips in the center of the table. "What a day! Nothing has gone right. I had a showing scheduled this morning, but the woman who's been bugging me to look at this adorable redone ranch *cancelled* because she said she had to take her daughter to the emergency room!"

Max looked around at the group. A few looked shocked, but the rest smirked at each other.

Buzzy smiled at her. "Well, I'm glad you could make it, Rita. I didn't know you were joining us this weekend. Did you reserve a site?"

Rita tore open the bag of chips and chose one to scoop up a glob of dip from Becky's plate. "Thanks. I'm famished. I didn't get breakfast because I was busy staging that house. And then she doesn't show up! No, I didn't reserve a spot. I brought my tent and thought I can just set it up on one of your sites. They allow that in this park." She looked around at the others.

No one spoke for a moment, and then Becky offered. "I think we have room, don't we, Greg?" Her husband shrugged slightly and then nodded.

"Great," Rita said while she loaded another chip with dip. "And when I packed my car, I couldn't find the tent stakes. Maybe someone has something I can use?"

Greg nodded again. "I think we have stakes for our screen room. We don't *have* to put it up if you need the stakes." More eye rolls from the group.

"Perfect! So what have I missed?"

Buzzy said, "I was just starting to say when you arrived that the campground hostess told me there's been some break-ins around here—just small things missing—but she suggests we lock our campers anytime we're away from them."

"In the campground?" Carole got up to pass around the brownies and ice cream.

"But I can't lock my tent!" Rita said. She shook her head in exasperation and got up to fill a plate.

A young blond woman sitting at the end of the table said, "Wait! What?"

Buzzy repeated the information.

"Do they think it's kids?" Becky asked.

"I don't think they have any idea," Buzzy said.

Patrice had been listening from the next table. "I can't imagine what they would want out of our campers." She laughed. "Most of us have furnished them by dumpster diving and hitting the thrift shops."

"But some of our things have sentimental value. Things I wouldn't want to lose anyway," Leah Groton said. Max thought of the chandelier made from Leah's mother's jewelry.

"Well, we just need to be careful," Buzzy said.

Rita returned to the table with an overflowing plate and wiggled in between Becky and Carole.

Carole indicated Max and Lil. "Rita, these are my sisters — Lil from Kansas and Max from Colorado. They're staying with me this weekend. Ladies, this is Rita Fearn. From Des Moines, right Rita?"

Rita, with her mouth full, nodded and gave a little wave of her hand.

Buzzy stood and announced to the whole group, "The campfire tonight will be down the hill by the lake. We have permission from the rangers to use one of the fire pits at an empty tent site down there. Greg has firewood in his truck. Bring your own lawn chairs. And we'll initiate Brooke into the group."

Leah added, "Patrice is bringing her guitar so we'll have a good old fashioned campfire sing."

There was a smattering of applause as several got up and started to pack up their dishes. Max and Lil joined Carole to help Buzzy put away the food. Max got a glimpse of the inside of Buzzy's camper when she took a bowl of coleslaw in to store in the fridge. White beadboard paneling, aqua and light green cushions, and fish patterned pillows gave a fresh, crisp feeling.

"It's starting to get chilly," Carole said to her sisters. "I hope you brought sweatshirts or jackets."

"Of course," Lil told her. "We *were* raised by the same mother, remember?"

"'You don't have to wear it if you don't need it. Just have it along,'" Carole quoted in a sing-song voice and they all laughed.

As they walked back to Carole's camper, Max asked, "So what does Patrice teach?"

"Elementary music and she has a nice voice. She lost her husband in a car accident."

"There's more young members than I expected," Lil said. "Mostly at the other tables."

Carole nodded. "The redhead with the single braid? That's Brooke Hurlbut. She's a teacher too—special ed, I think—but her husband is a greenskeeper at a golf course. So he's busiest in the summer and she loves to camp. They agreed if she was going to do it, she'd have to go it alone. She's the one that they're going to initiate tonight. Jessi has the long blonde hair and glasses. She's a physician's assistant. Her husband is an over-the-road trucker. If he's available, he comes with her. He must be on the road this time. Sophie, the short blonde, is single. She's a lawyer and in the state legislature. So she can only join us if the assembly isn't in session."

"Wow, quite a variety," Lil said.

They were silent for a few moments, enjoying the pleasant evening. Dusk was descending and fireflies drifted up from the tall grass along the road.

Then Max said, "Rita seems kind of high maintenance."

"Yes, she's one of those people who decides she's coming on the spur of the moment and never has everything she needs. All of us borrow from each other if we need something, but it's like Rita doesn't plan *except* to borrow. When she brings her camper, she forgets to get water or something's wrong with it, and she's always looking for someone to help her." Carole shook her head in frustration.

They reached Carole's campsite. "But, they are a great group—lots of fun and very interesting." Carole stopped. "Maybe we should go in one at a time to get our stuff—avoid injuries, you know." She grinned, and then turned more serious. "Max, I think one of us should drive down to the beach. The path is pretty treacherous. There's lots of roots and some loose rock. I'm afraid that,

25

especially with it getting dark, Lil will wreck her new knee."

"Fine with me," Max said. "I'm not anxious to try something like that either. Think it's okay if I take Rosie along?"

"I don't know why not. I'll be right out." She took the ice cream and the container of leftover brownies in, and soon reappeared with a jacket and a bottle of water.

CHAPTER THREE

CAROLE RODE in the back seat of Max's little car with Rosie and, as they left the campground, gave directions to turn left on the beach road, heading away from the park entrance.

The beach was small and tapered to the northwest, bookended by a beach house with a round tower at the north end and a picnic shelter at the south. The buildings were constructed of stone and timber by the Civilian Conservation Corps in the 1930s. The architecture of these buildings had long fascinated Max, but she resisted the temptation to explore until later. There was a lovely view of the lake, and firepits were spaced along the beach, one with a tent beside it.

Once out of the car, Max helped Carole get the lawn chairs out of the trunk. By the time they had them set up, Buzzy and the young woman Jessi had a bonfire going. Laughter and insults flew around the circle as the other campers set up chairs and rearranged them. The sisters moved their chairs next to Lois. A few small children played in the sand. Firelight brought a glow to faces as stars began to appear in the fading day, and small waves at the lake edge gently lapped the beach.

Rosie was an instant hit, going from person to person looking to be petted or scratched. Brooke Hurlbut was especially taken with the dog.

"She thinks you're sisters, Brooke," Sophie laughed. "You know because of your hair color."

"I could have uglier sisters," Brooke said, and leaned down to scratch the dog behind both ears. "Right, girl?"

Carole looked at Max and laughed. "No comments, okay?"

Greg was unloading the rest of the firewood from his truck into a folding wagon. "I talked to a ranger when I was buying more firewood. He said most of the break-ins have been in unlocked campers and a few at unlocked farm homes in the area."

"So if we locked up, we should be okay?" Leah asked.

"Sounds like it."

Rita tripped on a branch outside the circle and stumbled into the group. "Whoops!" she laughed. She looked around and slapped her forehead. "I forgot a lawn chair!"

Greg stood up. "Here, take mine."

"Then where will you sit, Greg?" Buzzy asked.

He grabbed an unsplit log and turned it on end. "This will be fine."

"Great!" Rita said, and plopped down in Greg's chair.

"Notice she didn't offer to take the log," Carole whispered to her sisters.

Conversation and laughter swirled around the campfire while Patrice got out her guitar and tuned it. Finally, she said, "We'll start with *'She'll be Comin' 'Round the Mountain'* with our special words."

Max and Lil sang along with the first verse but then faded out as the rest of the group shouted out the second.

> *She'll be pullin' a silver Airstream when she comes*
> *She'll be pullin' a silver Airstream when she comes*
> *She'll be pullin' a silver Airstream*
> *She'll be pullin' a silver Airstream*
> *She'll be pullin' a silver Airstream when she comes*

The next verse was the traditional "We will all go out and meet her when she comes" so Max and Lil joined in again. Verse four started out:

> *We'll all bring out our cowbells when she comes…*

And a huge din broke out as almost all of the women pulled out cowbells of varying sizes and started ringing them. The kids in the circle giggled at their mothers and grandmothers carrying on. Buzzy got up and ushered Brooke to the center of the circle by the fire and the group finished the verse. At the end, they shouted in unison, "Welcome Brooke!"

Between the firelight and the attention, Brooke's face was almost as red as her hair. Rosie was cowering under Max's chair. Max muttered to Lil, "I should have brought ear plugs for her."

Brooke bowed and said "Thank you all. I will try to be a good member." They cheered and whistled. Several got up and hugged her.

After a few minutes, Patrice rung her cowbell again. "Ladies!" She turned to Greg and two other men sitting on one side. "And Gentlemen. Let's get back to our singing."

They cruised through several oldies: *Moonlight Bay, By the Light of the Silvery Moon,* and *Let Me Call You Sweetheart.* Max, Lil, and Carole, although none of them were ever known for their vocal talents, added the verse that they had learned at youth camp decades before:

Don't you call me Sweetheart
I don't love you any more
Since I caught you necking
With the girl next door.
I will find another
Who will take your place
Don't you call me Sweetheart
Or I'll slap your face.

More whistles and applause followed their performance. "Obviously not much discriminating taste here," Max commented to her sisters.

Babs was sitting next to Lil and leaned over her to whisper to Carole, "I'm going to go back up. I feel a migraine coming on."

Carole nodded and patted her hand. "Just leave your chair. We'll bring it up in the car."

"Or would you like a ride?" Max asked.

Babs shook her head slightly. "No, thank you. That's not necessary. It would be great if you just bring the chair." She got up and skirted the back of the group to the path.

Rita jumped up, knocking over the light weight chair. "I'll walk up with you. I haven't got my tent set up yet." She ignored the collapsed chair and caught up with Babs. As they headed up the path, the group could still hear Rita's shrill voice going a mile a minute. Greg set the chair back up and sat down, shaking his head as he did so.

One of the kids clamored for s'mores, so Buzzy got out marshmallows and roasting sticks. While the children and a few adults brandished the long forks, occasionally turning a soft white confection into a flaming torch for a few seconds, Patrice continued with several solo numbers. She finished with *Could I Have This Dance?*, the Anne Murray classic.

Max heard a small gasp from Carole, who was sitting between her and Lil.

Carole had her hand over her mouth and tears pooled in her eyes. Max took her ˋsister's other hand. "What's the matter?" she whispered.

On the other side, Lil put her arm around Carole's shoulders. "This was Bob's favorite song," Carole said softly. "He always sang along when we danced."

Lil hugged her. "I'm so sorry."

Carole noticed others looking at her and quickly wiped her eyes. "Some things kind of sneak up on you,"

31

she whispered to Max and Lil. "I read a quote once that the original loss was like an earthquake, pulling your foundations out from under you, but later there's always aftershocks to deal with, like this." She smiled at the others and fluttered her fingers to indicate that she was okay. With effort, she listened to the rest of the song, gripping her sisters' hands.

"Thank you, Patrice," Buzzy said. "That was wonderful. Tomorrow morning, whoever wants to tour the round barn, meet at my camper at 10:00."

Everyone folded up chairs and cleaned up around the site. Max noticed a couple of the women talking to Patrice and glancing over toward Carole. A shadow passed over Patrice's face, and she headed toward Carole.

"Carole, they said that last song upset you. I'm sorry. I know your husband's death is fairly recent, but I had no idea…"

Carole reached and took her hand. "How could you know? Please don't give it another thought. Besides, in the end it was a nice reminder. You sang it beautifully."

"I hope so. Thank you for understanding. Believe me, I know what you're feeling."

Carole waved it off. "It's bound to happen. I hope we get to hear you sing again while we're here."

"Maybe the last night. See you tomorrow?"

"Absolutely."

Patrice went to put away her guitar, and Carole turned to help Max and Lil pack up the chairs.

BACK AT THE CAMPSITE, Max got the lawn chairs out of the car while Carole opened up the trailer.

A few minutes after she stepped inside, she yelled. "Oh, no!"

"What's the matter?" Lil hobbled up the steps into the camper.

"My power's off," Carole answered. She opened the freezer door of the fridge to a mass of dripping ice cream. "Oh, man," She grabbed the carton and hauled it, still dripping, to the sink. "I'd better check the power post. But I screwed up. I had the fridge set on electric instead of auto. Then it would have switched to propane if the electricity wasn't working."

She hurried around to the back of the trailer. Soon she returned. "I don't think the power post is working at all."

"But there're lights on in your camper," Lil said.

"Those run off the 12 volt battery. I need to talk to the host. Be right back." Carole grabbed her phone to use as a flashlight and hurried up the road. Max and Lil looked at each other and shrugged since neither of them had any experience with a camper.

Because of the curve in the road, Carole soon disappeared. A few lights had been left on in the trailers that they could see, and most had decorative outdoor lights outlining the tops or edges of their awnings.

Max and Lil sat at the picnic table while they waited.

"This camping seems like an awful lot of hassle," Max commented. "I mean, I love the outdoors and I do a lot of nature hikes, but give me a nice hotel room at the end of the day."

"You know, for the oldest of five children, you're kind of a spoiled brat," Lil said.

"Oh, hush. I've earned it."

The wind was picking up and a few leaves swirled around the campsite. The quarter moon occasionally hid behind some high sailing clouds. They sat silently for a few minutes, listening to the sounds of cicadas and the wind in the trees. A cry for help down the road snapped them back to attention.

"Is that Carole?" Lil asked, lumbering to her feet. She leaned on the table to get her new knee over the bench.

"No, that's from the other direction." Max had already started down the road, but turned back to put Rosie on her leash. "Why don't you wait here for Carole?"

"That's probably a good idea so Carole knows where you went."

Max was off, walking quickly. The wind seemed to be stirred more by her passage. She rounded the corner and saw Leah Groton's pink and white confection of a camper. Leah sat in a pink webbed lawn chair, her head in her hands.

"Hi," Max said. It sounded too casual, but she didn't see any problem or threat. "Did you yell for help?"

Leah looked up and nodded. "I did," she said, her voice barely above a whisper.

"What happened?"

"Someone was in my camper."

Max sat at the picnic table. "How do you know?"

"My chandelier is gone. And the pink telephone and a couple of other things."

"Did you have it locked?" Max remembered Leah asking if locking up would avoid a break-in.

Leah dropped her head. "I did. But I forgot my jacket and went back for it. I don't remember locking it the second time."

Max pulled her phone out of her pocket. "I'm going to call 911."

Leah snapped her head up. "Oh, I don't think that's necessary. I — "

"Yes, it is," Max said, and dialed. She described what happened and assured the dispatcher that no one was hurt or threatened at the time. She gave them the campsite number and hung up.

When Max got off the phone, Leah said, "I told you that my sister hadn't spoken to me in years. That's not quite true." She stared off in the distance and wrung her hands. "I get emails and voicemails occasionally that are very bitter and almost threatening. Like saying she hopes I'm dead." She picked at her fingernails and then looked at Max. "She might have done this."

"Then she needs help."

"Yes, she does. I'm sure she has mental issues. But I *don't* want the police involved."

Max scratched her head and yawned. It was getting late. "Look at it this way. If your sister has a vendetta against you, would she be likely to break into other campers and houses?"

"Maybe not. I don't know—I can't explain any of her behavior any more."

"I suppose it's none of my business, but my sisters will tell you that has never stopped me. Are you married, Leah?"

Leah shook her head. "Divorced. A couple of years ago. It was amicable, but he just wasn't ready to settle down. That sounds trite but it was true."

"Other women?"

"No. Not that I know of anyway. He wanted to live the college life, party to the wee hours, drink himself into oblivion. That sort of thing. I preferred quiet evenings at home with an occasional dinner out. I think we're both much happier."

Max nodded. "I understand. My marriage only lasted ten years and the last five were an effort. When you're young and living the college life, you don't often know what your long term interests will be. It turned out we had almost nothing in common."

A white police SUV with blue and yellow lettering pulled slowly along the road. Max stood, stepped toward the headlights where she could be seen, and waved her arms. The car rolled to a stop. A slight middle-forties man with thinning reddish hair in a comb over stepped out with a notebook in hand.

Max, of course, took charge. "Hi, I'm Maxine Berra. I'm the one who called. And this is Leah Groton. Someone stole things from her camper while we were at a campfire down at the beach."

The man nodded. "Officer Bryant. Can you tell me what happened?" He looked at Leah.

"Like Max said, we were down at the beach for a campfire. I had locked my camper once but came back for a jacket and think I forgot to relock it."

"About what time did you find things missing?"

Leah looked at Max. "Probably half an hour ago or so, wouldn't you say?"

"That sounds about right." Max looked up the road at the sound of footsteps. A flashlight bobbed along, hiding Carole and Lil until they reached the circle of light cast by Leah's trailer lamps.

"What's going on?" Carole called out.

"Another burglary," Max said when they got nearer. "Someone was in Leah's trailer while we were at the campfire."

"Oh no!" Carole grabbed Leah in a hug. "Are you okay?"

"They were gone by the time I got here," Leah said. She explained about forgetting to lock the trailer the second time. "They took the pink phone, that flamingo fan, and my chandelier."

Lil groaned. "And your chandelier was so special. How —?"

"Ladies!" Officer Bryant interrupted. "I would like to get Ms. Groton's story."

"Oh, sorry," Lil said. "We'll stay out of your way." She pulled Carole over to sit on the other side of the picnic table. Carole mimed zipping her lips. Fortunately, Officer Bryant wasn't looking.

He had turned back to Leah. "You said a phone and light fixture are missing?"

Leah nodded.

"Were they hard wired?"

"No, the phone was just for show. The chandelier was mounted on a ring that fit around the light."

"I'll have to check that out if you don't mind."

Leah shrugged. "Please do."

"Would you come and show me where the items were?" Bryant asked.

"Certainly." Leah got up and led him to the camper.

While they were inside, Max turned to Carole. "What did you find out about the power post?"

Carole sighed. "As I suspected, no one will look at it until tomorrow. The campground host's job is just to pass the message on. We'll be fine. The lights and the water pump will still work off the battery. Luckily we don't need the AC."

"What about the refrigerator?" Lil asked.

"I switched it to propane. This burglary is really unsettling. Why would someone take those things?"

The camper door opened and Officer Bryant came back out, followed by Leah. They were both laughing. Bryant was much more attractive without his stern look.

Bryant closed his notebook and stuck it in his pocket. Leah looked more relaxed than she had all evening and, when the officer turned to say he would be in touch, she gave him a warm smile. Lil looked at Carole and raised her eyebrows.

The officer pulled away in his cruiser, and Leah returned to join the others at the picnic table.

"Nice guy," Leah, pushing a shock of her short dark hair away from her forehead. "He said the items are unusual enough to be easily spotted if they show up in thrift or pawn shops."

"Well, be sure and lockup when you go in tonight," Max said.

Carole added, "Max likes to boss us around, but that is good advice."

Max stuck out her tongue at Carole, who said "Are you going to be all right alone? I could stay here with you tonight if you like."

Leah waved her hand. "No, no. I'll be fine. Officer Bryant said they will have a patrol car cruise through several times tonight." She got up from the table. "Thanks for your help."

"We didn't do much, but you're welcome. Did you tell him about your sister?" Max asked.

Leah shook her head. "I just can't. It's been a long day, and I'm ready for sleep."

"Right," Lil said. "I think we all are."

THE THREE SISTERS TRUDGED back up the road to Carole's trailer. Max told the others what Leah had said about her sister Tammy.

"Who's sleeping where?" Max wanted to know.

"We can either draw straws, or Lil and I can take the dinette bed and you can have the couch," Carole said.

"That sounds good to me," Max said. "Lil's a more sound sleeper than I am."

It took a lot of jockeying to get the beds made up and each of them ready for bed. Max tossed and turned, feeling the springs of the jackknife couch through the sheets. Lil tried to avoid disturbing Carole while she looked for a comfortable position for her knee. And Carole worried that no one was going to get any sleep. But eventually they did.

CHAPTER FOUR

WHEN MAX WOKE UP, it was still dark out. That was not unusual for her, but tonight it seemed like she had hardly been asleep. She shifted on the couch trying to get comfortable enough to nod off again, but she heard voices. Not yelling, exactly, but with a strident note. She groped for her phone and checked the time. 2:30. The voices continued, and a truck motor started up.

She grabbed a hoodie from the foot of the bed and swung her legs over the edge, searching for her flip flops. Immediately a wet nose poked her in the leg. "Rosie!" she whispered. "Out of my way."

Taking her phone as a flashlight, she moved as quietly as she could to the door. Rosie seemed to take up most of the floor space, making it difficult to navigate. The lock took a little fiddling with, but finally she got it open. Rosie nearly knocked her over trying to beat her out the door. The dog was not silent going down the steps but fortunately didn't take off barking. Max stepped out of the camper and tried to quietly close the door, hearing the latch click.

As Max hooked the leash to Rosie's collar and moved toward the edge of the road and around the next camper, she could see several women across the road at Babs' spot. Flashlights illuminated some of the area. The wind caused branches to click and rub together insistently, and Max pulled her hoodie tighter. The spotty light from the flashlights revealed a lumpy figure hunched at the picnic table, another bent over the first, and two others in earnest conversation, but she couldn't recognize any faces or even identify gender.

Where was Babs' camper? A pickup sat there, but there was nothing behind it. She spotted Leah.

"What's happening?"

Leah pointed toward the back of the site. The front of Babs' camper was barely visible amongst the trees and shrubs in the dark. Max hadn't even noticed it when she first looked.

"Babs' camper rolled backwards. There's a little gully behind the site."

"Omigosh! Was she in it?"

Leah nodded. "She's over there at the picnic table. Has a little gash in her head but otherwise seems okay."

"Does that happen often?"

"It shouldn't *ever* happen. I helped her set up, and I *know* we put the wheel chocks in. Someone must have pulled them out and given the trailer a little push. There's one of the chocks over to the side." She indicated a bright yellow, curved piece of heavy plastic laying in the grass.

Max gasped. "Who would do that?"

"I don't know." A flashing red and blue light lit up the road and gave a surreal cast to all of the faces. "Here come the police." She led Max back to the picnic table area.

Jessi, clad in striped men's pajamas, was wiping Babs' forehead and preparing bandages. A large man in a tee shirt and blue plaid pajama bottoms stood, hands on hips, talking to Brooke. Patrice had been sitting in the old pickup at the front of Babs' site. She got out and approached the police car.

"What is Patrice doing?" Max asked Leah.

"She is going to hook up the camper and pull it back where it belongs after the police check it out. The camper was stopped by that big oak tree."

"Heavens!" Max pulled in Rosie's leash as the dog struggled to greet the newcomers. "Is there anything I can do to help?"

Leah shook her head. "Not until the police are done. We may need help hooking up and moving that camper since it's so dark."

"I'm not trying to be sarcastic—honest—but do you always have this much drama at these gatherings?"

"Never." Leah looked around at the scene. "I mean someone might be going through personal problems—with their kids, jobs, marriages—and we all try to lend support. But not these threatening situations."

Carole joined the group. "What's going on?" Leah repeated the story.

Carole's face changed from curiosity to horrified. "That's awful! She could have been killed!"

Brooke walked up to them and heard Carole's remark. "She was very lucky."

"But it must have been intentional…" Carole said.

Leah hugged herself for warmth, and perhaps reassurance, in the night chill. "No doubt about it. There's no other explanation. Who is that guy you were talking to, Brooke?"

"Herbert or Albert or—Lambert, I think that's it. He's in that big fifth wheel in that other loop. Said he couldn't sleep and was watching TV when he heard the trailer hit the tree."

Max walked over to the picnic table and sat down across from Babs. Rosie laid her head on Babs' knee in her own form of comfort.

"How are you doing?" Max asked.

Babs slowly shook her head, grimacing with the pain. "I dunno. Why—*why* are they blaming me? I had nothing to do with it." But she noticed Rosie, and she relaxed slightly as she caressed the dog's silky fur.

"It?" Max asked, although she thought she knew.

"My husband was accused of embezzling money from his clients. And he's in prison—he's being punished for it. But he says he didn't do it and I believe him. They said he even stole from my mother. He wouldn't do that —he loves my mom!" Her breath caught in a little sob. "But I was stupid. I was part of the problem. For years we lived the high life. I spent money like there was no end."

"Why do you think that's the reason behind this?"

"I've gotten email threats, apparently from some of the people who think he embezzled their money. The police haven't been able to trace them. I don't know what they want from me. That camper and truck are all I have besides my little apartment."

Max rubbed her shoulder. "You need to go to an ER to get checked out."

"No, I don't want to."

Max smiled at her. "We'll see about that."

She studied the woman as others came up to check on her. Babs declared her husband's innocence, but blamed herself for the need for money. If Babs' husband didn't do the embezzling, why was she rationalizing it? And if her mother was a victim too, that must cause conflicting loyalties.

Patrice finished her conversation with the police and returned to Babs' truck. A female officer got out of the cruiser and walked over to the picnic table.

"Thank you for coming," Babs said quietly.

"I assume you are Ms. Grangersmith?" the officer said, indicating the bandage on Babs' forehead. "Can you tell me what happened?"

Babs shrugged. "I don't really know. I was sound asleep. When I woke up, I was moving, but you know how it is—I didn't know where I was or what was going on, and then the camper hit the tree. The bed is by the back wall, so it was quite a jolt. I don't remember anything after that until Leah pounded on the door."

"One of the women said this had to have been done deliberately. How do you know that?"

"Leah and I have talked about that. She helped me set up, and we both remember we put the chocks in. Besides, if we hadn't, they would have still been in the storage compartment and not on the ground."

Max thought at least Babs' thinking processes didn't seem to be affected.

"And do you have any idea who might have done this?"

Babs began to recount the story of her husband's troubles and the threats she had been receiving. Max gave Babs a little nod and got up to join the others by the pickup.

Carole said to her, "Jessi is going to take Babs to the hospital when the police are done. We may need extra help to pull the camper out if they can't get the truck close enough to hook up."

Max looked a little surprised at the plan, but Carole patted her on the arm. "Don't worry, old lady. If you don't feel up to it, there's plenty of young blood here."

Max huffed. "I'll do what I can. I'm not *that* old."

"We'll see." Carole grinned.

"Your insults aside, this is really disturbing. Someone wandering around breaking into campers and houses and someone else messing with campers in the middle of the night."

"Maybe it's the same person," Carole said.

"Doesn't seem likely—not if the attack on Babs is related to her husband's crimes, or at least what he's accused of. She claims he's not guilty. But, why would they pick on anyone else?"

"As a distraction? Maybe that's far-fetched, but it seems just as likely as two totally separate crime sprees in the same little campground."

"You have a point."

Buzzy, who had gone back to her camper, returned carrying a large work light and a heavy-duty extension cord. She set it on the ground next to the pick up. "We're going to need to shed a little light on our work."

"Maybe I don't get it, but why not just call a towing service?"" Max asked.

"Cost, for one thing. Babs is pretty strapped for funds. Besides those little campers aren't that heavy, so if we can just get it a little ways back up the slope, we can hook the truck up. Let's go take a look at the back."

Max led Rosie and followed Buzzy, using her phone to light the way and avoid any potholes or gopher mounds. A young man in a navy police jacket already had a spotlight on the area and was taking photographs. He looked at them, nodded, and continued with his task.

The back end of the trailer was wedged against the trunk of the old oak. A protruding branch had added a crease to the top.

"Well, it doesn't look like much, but it will be expensive to fix." Buzzy shook her head in disgust as she surveyed the damage. "The frame is probably bent," she added.

"Does she have insurance?" Max asked.

"Let's hope so." Buzzy turned and trudged back up the hill. "We'll need to gather some ropes and straps. Most of the girls carry them," she said over her shoulder. By the time they returned to the picnic table area, Lois and Sophie had joined the group. Buzzy told them what they were going to need and Brooke, Sophie, and Patrice offered to round them up.

"I have several lariats that should do the trick." Patrice grinned. "They aren't just for looks, you know."

Buzzy turned to Lois. "Babs is going to need somewhere else to sleep when Jessi brings her back, even if we get her trailer pulled back up. Do you have room?"

"Sure. I can make the dinette into a bed. I'll go do that."

"Do you need help?" Max asked.

"That would be great. But you almost have to be a gymnast to make up the beds in these things," Lois said.

As they walked back up the hill, Max said, "Lil and I really appreciate what you've done for our sister. She seems to really enjoy it. Not my cup of tea, but to each her own."

"Like hotels better, right?"

"You got it." She tied Rosie's leash to the leg of Lois' picnic table and followed Lois inside.

Max moved the cushions off the benches as Lois directed. Lois reached under the table to flip a latch to raise the table leg so that she could lower the top to be level with the benches. They arranged the cushions to cover the now flat surface and Lois pulled sheets from a cupboard over the dinette. It was a challenge getting the fitted sheet over the back corners. Lois pulled the corners up while Max, with a couple of grunts and groans, managed to capture the cushions in the obstinate sheet.

Lois added blankets from another cubbyhole. It did amaze Max the way every square inch of these little tin cans was utilized.

"I don't have any extra pillows, but we can check Babs' trailer and use hers. Or someone else probably has an extra." Lois brushed her hands on her sweat pants and pushed her hair back, as she turned to Max. "I'm a little worried about Carole. She does well on these trips, but she's awfully depressed at home."

Max had her hand on the door latch but turned with surprise. "Really? She always seems pretty upbeat when I talk to her on the phone."

Lois nodded. "She's good at covering up. But I've stopped there when she's just sitting and staring, or even crying. She doesn't want to stay on the farm, but doesn't know what she wants to do."

"I know. She's talked about that. I've suggested that she come out to Colorado and live with me. But she's lived in Castleroll her whole life, and she doesn't want to move."

"She has a daughter there, doesn't she?"

"Yes, Annie. And I understand that, I guess." Max shrugged. Actually, she couldn't really understand why someone wouldn't want to try a new place ever. She had left their home town after high school for college and never moved back. "But I had no clue that she was that depressed."

"I just thought you and your sister should know."

"Thank you. I'm glad you told me."

"Thank you for your help. I'll check Babs' trailer for pillows."

When they returned to Babs' site, Carole told Max that she and Lil would go back to her camper. "I don't see us pushing a beached trailer," she said.

Patrice was backing the truck down to the camper. Buzzy stood to the side of the trailer hitch giving her hand signals. "Whoa!" she yelled, as she threw up a hand to signal to stop.

"Whoa?" Brooke laughed.

Buzzy grinned. "Hey, she's a cowgirl, isn't she?"

Patrice smirked at them out the driver's window. Buzzy deftly fastened the hitch and signaled Patrice to move forward.

"Giddyup!" Patrice yelled as she threw the truck in drive and began to edge it back up the hill. Once it was back in place, she put the emergency brake on and swung down out of the truck. "We'll just leave it hooked up so it can't happen again."

Lois said "I'm going to get a pillow for her out of there. We probably should empty her fridge too. Leah, why don't you see if there's an empty tote in one of the outside compartments?"

Patrice handed Leah the ring of keys with a small silver one separated out. "In case they're locked, use Babs' keys to check those compartments?". We'll see what else needs to come out of the camper. She'll want her clothes and toiletries, at least." Patrice and the others, except for Max, returned to the door side of the camper.

The bobbing flashlights and uneven ground made Max nervous. She carefully followed Leah to check the compartments. Leah tried the one furthest front. "This one isn't locked." She peered in with a flashlight. "But it's just water hoses." She moved toward the back, opening and closing each cubbyhole. Finally, in the back, she pulled out a small plastic tub. "This is where she keeps her power cord when she travels…" She stopped and pulled an object out of the tote. It was a pink telephone. She looked at Max, her mouth open and an expression of shock on her face.

Max gently took the phone from her. "What else is in there?" Leah bent back over the opening with the flashlight. "The fan. I don't see the chandelier," her voice came back. She pulled out the items and, after thinking a moment and looking around, instructed Max, "Follow

51

me." She took the phone from Max and put the fan and the phone in the weeds at the edge of the woods.

"Please don't say anything," she said. "I want to talk to Babs first about it. If I don't get the chance, tomorrow morning, I'll get them and say they must have been dropped there by the thief. I'm sure there's an explanation, and Babs doesn't need any more on her plate. Will you keep it a secret for now?"

Max nodded. "For now." She was hesitant, but agreed that Babs didn't need any accusations right at this time. However, it bothered her that Babs had left the campfire before the others. She had the opportunity to raid Leah's camper.

Max and Leah took the empty tote around to the other side of the camper where the women were bringing out clothing, a laptop, and a couple of plastic bags of items. Buzzy took the tote from Leah.

"Thanks. I'll get the perishables out of the fridge and move them to mine."

"Is there anything I can do?" Max asked.

"I think we've got it handled," Buzzy answered. "Thanks for your help."

Max nodded. "In that case, I think I'll head back to bed."

"I won't be far behind you."

Carole and Lil were just getting into bed. Max still had her pajamas on, so stripped off her hoodie, dropped it on the floor, and fell into bed. She expected to immediately fall asleep but tossed and turned, consumed by the dilemma of Leah's discovery.

Chapter Five

MAX WOKE UP the next morning to sunshine and no smell of coffee. She lay there a while recalling the events of the previous night — really just a few hours ago. With effort, she pushed herself to a sitting position and gradually eased herself out of bed. Carole and Lil were still asleep, soft snores coming from one of them. She slipped on her shoes and hoodie. Rosie, stretched on the floor, groaned and went back to sleep. So much for a guard dog.

Since Rosie wasn't clamoring for a walk and no one else was up, now would be a good time for a shower. Max gathered a towel, soap, and shampoo and headed up the road to the campground shower house. Lights were on in a few campers, but no one was outside. The morning sun was bright in the spots that it made it through the trees.

The shower room had four stalls. A damp, musty smell greeted her. There was no one else there. The place looked fairly clean in spite of the odor. She entered the first stall. The small cubicle had a vertical half wall dividing the actual shower from a dressing area. A skimpy plastic curtain missing a couple of hooks hung haphazardly in the shower opening.

The dressing area contained a wooden bench and one small hook. She slipped off her shoes and put them under the bench, hung her towel on the hook, and placed her folded pajamas and hoodie on the bench.

The small built-in soap dish in the shower itself had such a slant to it that when she set the shampoo and body wash on it, they tumbled to the floor. So she stood them on the floor in the corner.

Max examined the control under the nozzle. There was only a metal button with no temperature indications. She pushed the button and was hit by a blast of freezing cold water which drove her back into the corner. Fortunately, it shut off after a few seconds.

Would the water even get any hotter? She should have gotten a hotel room. She reached out and pushed the button again, holding it a little longer. This time it lasted about ten seconds and got a touch warmer. She continued to push the button until the temperature was tolerable. Alternating button pushes with suds, she managed to get her hair and self to some semblance of clean.

Her feelings of victory were short-lived when she pushed the curtain back and found water from the shower had run into the dressing area because of the slope of the floor. She had to stand in a half-inch of water to get dressed. And her clothes, towel and shoes were wet — so much for the shower curtain.

By the time she got back to the camper and changed into dry clothes, she really needed a cup of coffee. The power problem that Carole had discovered after the campfire meant that Carole's coffee pot would not be producing anytime soon. Surely one of the other Glampers had coffee perking by now. After all, how could it be 'glamorous camping' without coffee?

Max let herself out and found a mug in the utility table. She walked to the edge of the campsite and glanced up and down the road. Past Babs' camper and old truck, she saw Brooke Hurlbut's red hair glinting in the morning sun.

She headed down the road, mug in hand. Long shadows stretched across the road like fingers reaching for the golden spots of early sun filtering through the trees. It was a lovely morning.

Brooke looked up from straightening the tablecloth on her picnic table as Max approached. "Good morning," Brooke said, sounding a little strained.

"Good morning. It was a short night. I'm wondering if you have any coffee," Max said, holding up her mug. "Carole's power post went out last night, and we're waiting for someone to come fix it. After the night we had, I think I need a little caffeine. Or a lot."

"Absolutely. It's inside. I'll get it for you." She took Max's cup and was soon back with it full of steaming elixir.

Max wrapped both hands around the mug and inhaled deeply before taking a sip. "Excellent—thanks. How are you holding up this morning?"

Brooke looked around the campground. "It *was* quite a night, wasn't it? Poor Babs—I know she is so humiliated by what happened with her husband and is really hurting for money. Then all of this." She nodded toward the crumpled trailer.

"I can't imagine what someone is trying to gain," Max said.

"Just revenge. Just pure meanness."

Max nodded. "Seems like it. Do you think it was someone in the campground who did it?"

Brooke shrugged. "I doubt it. I can't believe it would be any of the women in our group. Babs lives near here, and I suppose a lot of people who were hurt by her husband's scheme are in the area. They would be close enough to do something like that."

"She told me last night that she believes her husband is innocent."

Brooke looked skeptical. "They usually say that, don't they?"

"I guess. It was great how everyone pulled together though."

"That's one of the things I love about camping and this group, especially," Brooke said. "But, almost anywhere people are willing to help. Even that guy from the other loop, Lambert Bardsley, was a big help getting the trailer hooked up back up."

"I noticed him," Max said. "I guess I was kind of surprised, because we saw him before supper sitting outside with his wife—I assume it was his wife. It looked like they were having quite an argument. And there's a 'For Sale' sign on his camper."

"I saw that," Brooke said.

Max sipped some more coffee. "He didn't look like he would be friendly to anyone. So how did you get involved with this group?"

"Patrice dragged me into it. We teach in the same school over in Bolt City." She smiled. "It's a fun group."

A DNR pickup drew their attention back to Carole's site. A guy dressed in work clothes got out and headed to the back of the site.

"He must be going to check the electrical post. I'd better go see if Carole's up. Thanks for the brew." Max held up her mug in kind of a salute.

"No problem. How about a refill?"

"That would be great. Tide me over until Carole has some going."

Brooke took the mug in and returned it steaming again. "Here you go. I'll be over in a bit."

When Max reached the camper, Carole was just coming outside. Rosie was right behind her, almost knocking her to the ground.

Carole spotted the truck. "Oh, good. Maybe we'll be able to have some coffee soon." Then she noticed Max's mug and smiled. "You've been out begging already this morning, I see."

"Brooke took pity on me. There aren't many things I'll beg for, but coffee is one of them." Max got one of the lawn chairs out from under the camper, shook it open, and sat down.

Carole walked around the camper to the electrical post to talk to the maintenance guy.

Rosie raced over to her mistress and laid her head on Max's knee with a soulful gaze."I suppose you're ready for a walk?"

Rosie pranced and panted, pushing her nose against Max's leg for emphasis. While Max was hooking up the leash, Carole returned.

She pumped her fist in the air. "Yes! He's got it fixed. Now for coffee and then I can make breakfast."

Max took Rosie for a short walk while Carole prepared French toast and sausage over a fire. When Max rounded the curve in the road, the campground looked different. Then she realized Becky's 'gypsy trailer' was gone. Only Rita's tent was there, haphazardly surrounded by coolers and totes.

Puzzled, she continued back to Carole's. Lil was up and sitting at the table. Carole bent over the fire flipping golden pieces of French toast. Both were quiet and sad looking.

"What's the matter?" Max asked.

"Lois said Becky got a call in the night that her daughter had a miscarriage," Carole answered.

"Oh, no. I just noticed that their camper is gone."

Carole nodded. "I feel so sorry for her. They were so excited about their first grandchild. As anyone is." She put a plate of French toast on the table. Max refreshed her cup of coffee and sat down.

"So, you talked to Lois this morning? Did Babs get back from the hospital?" Max asked.

"Yeah, Jessi brought her back about 5:00 this morning. Lois said she was still sleeping—that was about twenty minutes ago."

"That's good," Lil said. "She had an awful day."

Max turned to Carole. "Do *you* think the trailer being pushed is related to Babs' husband? Disgruntled clients?"

"I don't know what else it would be. Babs is such a sweet person. I can't imagine that she has any enemies, and I believe her when she says she was completely in the dark about her husband's schemes."

Max doused her French toast with syrup, causing her sisters to grimace. She was thinking about the discoveries she and Leah made in the compartment of Babs' camper. That didn't jive with Babs being a 'sweet person.' She said, "But what could anyone hope to gain?"

Carole shook her head. "I don't know. Most of their assets were seized, so Babs really has no money. She went to work as a check-out clerk in her local grocery store."

"What about a prank? Kids might think it was funny—maybe they didn't even expect it to roll that far," Lil said.

"I was saying to Leah last night that there seems to be a lot of drama in this group. And I don't mean that facetiously. It's a function of the situations of many of the women. Things like illness and loss of spouse," Max said. "Maybe I should say trauma instead of drama. Drama sounds fake."

Carole passed the plate of sausage. "True. There are more widows and divorcees than in the average group. This group has been a way for a lot of us to deal with the sadness in our lives. I think we tend to invite friends to join when they have gone through a major life change. Like Lois invited me. I was at loose ends. And while the group certainly doesn't replace Bob, it helps me cope with the loneliness. And makes me laugh."

Lil took another piece of French toast. "After I finish this, I think I'll grab a shower."

"Well, good luck with that." Max proceeded to recount her mood-dampening experience.

Carole covered her mouth trying to choke back laughter. She shook her head. "I'm sorry. The image is hysterical."

"Gee, thanks."

"I know. There's quite a learning curve with campground showers."

A police cruiser drove slowly down the road. They waved but couldn't see the driver.

"Probably not the guy from last night. Different shift," Lil said. "Leah seemed interested in him."

Max said, "I noticed that. Tell me, what has to happen now as far as Babs' camper is concerned? She can't stay in it, can she?"

"No," Carole said. "We'll have to wait and see what she feels like doing. I'm sure Lois would be glad to have her if she wants to remain for the weekend. But her trailer will need to be towed somewhere."

Buzzy and Lois walked down the road toward them. "Good morning, ladies!"

"Whether it's a good morning remains to be seen," Carole said. "It was a pretty short night."

Buzzy agreed. "That it was."

"I have a fresh pot of coffee. Can I interest you in any?"

"I would love some," Buzzy said, "but I'll get it."

"It's on the table there, and there's mugs in the storage compartment underneath. Right side. There's also some French toast and sausage left. How about some of that?"

Both women declined. Buzzy said "Lois? How about coffee?"

"Sure."

"We were wondering what Babs will do with the camper," Max said. "Where is she from?"

"Bentonsville—about 30 miles from here," Lois said. "When she came back this morning, she mentioned towing it there later. But I doubt if she should be driving. I will probably tow it for her."

Buzzy sipped her coffee. "Great coffee! I'm available too. We're moving the round barn tour to this afternoon, to give everyone a chance to rest up from last night. Since Becky and Greg left, we won't be doing the place mat or wheel-bearing projects."

"Good idea," Lil said.

They watched a late model, plain-Jane silver compact car drive slowly through the campground. It disappeared around the bend into the other loop but soon was back. It pulled over at Carole's site and a tall thin man with dark hair touched by gray and a neatly trimmed goatee got out. His clothes, although casual, looked expensive—designer jeans, cashmere sweater, leather loafers. Sort of professorial, Max thought.

Carole looked puzzled. "Can we help you?"

"I hope so. I'm looking for Barbara Grangersmith. I think she's with this group?"

"Barbara? Oh, Babs! Yes, she is, but I don't think she's awake yet. We had kind of a rough night last night. Would you like some coffee?"

"If you don't mind me waiting, that would be great. I'm Owen Balzac, by the way."

Max got up to fill a mug for him.

Buzzy narrowed her eyes and scrutinized the man as he approached the picnic table. "Weren't you...?"

"Grayton's business partner? Yes, I was." He sat down.

Buzzy straightened and frowned. "Why are you looking for Babs?"

Max was surprised by Buzzy's aggressive attitude. She set the mug down in front of Balzac but kept her eyes on Buzzy.

"I heard from a friend who works at the ER that she was brought in last night with an injury. I just wanted to check on her and see if she needed anything."

Buzzy kept up her abrupt tone. "I thought you had nothing to do with the Grangersmiths—that you blamed them for your bankruptcy."

The rest of the women looked at each other, startled by Buzzy's outburst.

Balzac exhaled. "Grayton, yes. But I don't believe Barbara ever had any idea what he was up to. I've tried to help her when I can. What exactly happened last night?"

Lois blew her bangs off her forehead and sighed. "It was crazy. Someone pulled the chocks from her wheels and pushed the trailer down the hill. It crashed into a tree and that's how Babs injured her head."

Balzac's jaw dropped. "You're kidding! Were the police called?"

"Yes, they're investigating," Max said. "She's apparently gotten threats, too, although I can't imagine what anyone is trying to accomplish."

"Who would do that? Kids, do you think? Incredible what they—." He stopped and looked back down the campground road. He looked back at Max. "You mean they think it's connected to Grayton? Revenge or something?" He looked again down the road. "Have they questioned others in the campground?"

"We really don't know," Max said. "It was pretty late last night, but I imagine they will eventually. Why?"

Owen shrugged. "Well, I'm not really at liberty to say."

Max studied his face. So why did he bring it up? And why did he keep looking into the other part of the campground?

"Here comes Babs now," Lil said.

Lois jumped up and hurried to Babs' side. She seemed to be moving pretty well, but her hair stuck out at odd angles because of the bandage on her crown. Lois took her arm, and she reluctantly allowed herself to be led to a lawn chair. Once she was seated, she glanced around at the group, and her jaw dropped a little when she spotted Owen Balzac at the table.

"Owen! What are you doing here?" Her tone was much friendlier than Buzzy's.

"I heard from a friend at the ER what happened and just wanted to see if I could help."

"Thank you, but I think it's going to take a professional." Babs pointed down the road at her camper. "I need to tow it to Dapper Camper at Bolt City. I called them this morning, and they'll give me an estimate."

Lois shook her finger at Babs. "You aren't towing anything anywhere today. You have a head injury, woman!"

Owen raised a hand. "That's something I can do."

Babs laughed. "When have you ever towed anything? No offense, but —"

"I tow my boat, and I grew up on a farm. I pulled wagons with a tractor. I can tow it. And I have nothing on today. How soon do they want it there?"

65

"Oh, that would be great, Owen, thank you. If you're sure you want to take the time, I suppose Lois is right, I shouldn't try it yet, although this old noggin in pretty hard." Babs knocked her fist on her head, grimacing as she did so. "They said I could bring it any time."

"No problem. Can I leave my car where it is?"

"Umm," Carole said. "You should probably — "

Buzzy interrupted. "There's an overflow parking area down at the end of the loop. Just past Babs' camper."

Owen stood up and stroked his beard. "Thanks. Does the camper need to be hooked up? I can't tell from here."

Lois shook her head. "We left it hooked up last night after we pulled it up from the hillside. I can go down there and show you what the dealer needs to look at."

"Fine. I'll move my car and meet you there."

"I'll go with you," Babs told Lois. Balzac left to move his car, and the women headed down the road.

Buzzy watched them go and shook her head.

"What's the matter, Buzzy?" Max asked. "You seem to have reservations about Mr. Balzac."

"I don't trust him. He lost a lot when the firm closed down, and he's part of the lawsuit against the Grangersmiths."

"How do you know that?" Carole asked. "Was the list published?"

Buzzy was watching what was going on at Babs' site. "Well, it's public. I've seen the list.""

"He seems sincere about helping Babs, and she was pleased to see him," Lil said.

Buzzy shrugged. "I just think she should be careful."

Patrice and Brooke walked down the road. Brooke had a Labradoodle on a leash and Rosie perked up as they entered Carole's campsite.

"Good morning!" Max said. "No wonder you got along so well with Rosie last night. I didn't realize you had your own dog along."

"Oh, this is Jessi's dog. I just offered to walk her. Jessi got back late from taking Babs to the ER and wants to catch a little more sleep."

"What's the dog's name?" Lil asked.

Brooke grinned. "Marilyn. She's a famous blonde, you know."

Patrice had been watching the activity down the road. "What's going on down at Babs' camper?"

"A friend is going to tow it to a dealer for repair estimates." Carole got up to refill her coffee.

"Friend?" Brooke asked. "One of our group?"

"Her husband's old business partner," Buzzy said with disgust.

"That must be awkward," Patrice said.

"She seems okay with it," Carole said. Babs' old pickup crept up the road pulling the creaking camper.

Owen Balzac nodded out the truck window at them. Lois and Babs walked behind the camper.

"It's a good thing that camper isn't worth much," Buzzy said. "I wouldn't put it past him to sell it and keep the money."

CHAPTER SIX

MAX THOUGHT IT WAS TIME to change the subject. She said to Patrice, "Brooke said you and she teach together?"

Patrice laughed. "Yes. She always says I tricked her into joining this group."

"How could she trick you?" Lil asked.

"I didn't expect to have so much fun," Brooke said.

Babs and Lois reached Carole's site and returned to their seats.

Babs refilled her coffee, eking out the last drops, and Carole took the pot inside to make fresh.

"That's a relief!" Babs said, returning to the table. "Oh, I know one of you would have taken it, but I hated to ask, and Owen seemed perfectly okay with doing it."

Buzzy frowned but made no comment.

"Have you been in contact with him since Grayton's trial?" Patrice asked.

Babs nodded. "He checks in on me occasionally. He's been helpful, just like today."

Max got up."I'm going to see if Carole needs any help."

Buzzy and Lois sat at the end of the table and talked in low voices, their heads bent over a park brochure. Lois looked up as Max approached.

"Going on the round barn tour this afternoon?"

Max said, "We haven't really talked about it. Too much else going on, I guess. Will there be much walking? You know about Lil's recent knee replacement, I think."

Lois nodded. "Yes, but it only takes about half an hour, and I think they have wheelchairs there."

Babs started to say some thing but stopped and rubbed her forehead.

A look of concern crossed Lois' face. "Are you okay, sweetie? That headache getting worse?"

Babs nodded. "I'd better go back and take one of those pills."

Lois got up. "I'll go with you. Maybe you should have a muffin or a little something to eat, too."

Babs let Lois help her up. "I should have run my camper down the hill earlier. I kind of like this being waited on."

Lois slapped her playfully on the shoulder. "Don't push it."

The rest of the group watched them go back up the road.

Buzzy was shaking her head. She said in a low voice to Max, "I don't want her to panic, but I wish she was a little more concerned about the situation. She isn't likely out of danger."

Max asked, "Do you think it's related to her husband?"

"What else could it be?"

Max shrugged. "Obviously, we know very little about it. But you mentioned the lawsuit. Do you know about how many people are involved in the suit?"

"I believe it's at least forty or fifty," Buzzy said.

"That many? Do you know most of those people?"

"Not really."

The man who had helped the night before, Lambert Bardsley, walked up the road from the other loop. He headed to their table. Brooke greeted him.

"Hi! Thanks for your help last night."

He nodded. "Sure. Glad to do something. How's your friend today? I see someone hauled the camper away."

"Yes, one of her friends took it to a dealer for her," Carole said.

"It looked like repairs will be extensive," Bardsley said.

Patrice agreed. "I'm afraid so. Can we offer you some coffee?"

He waved his hand. "No, no. My wife is fixing breakfast so I need to get back. Just wanted to check on things. Was your friend hurt?"

"A cut on the head," Carole said. "She just went to take a pain pill. We'll tell her you stopped."

71

"Thanks. I'll probably see you later." He headed back to his loop.

"Nice guy," Patrice said. "Did anyone get his name?"

Brooke swatted at a fly. "Lambert Bardsley."

Buzzy strained to look after him. "Really?"

Max frowned a little. "Why? Do you know him?"

Buzzy hesitated. "He's part of that lawsuit against Babs' husband, too. Are you all going on the tour this afternoon?"

Max looked at Lil. "I'm up for it. Are you?"

"I think so. It shouldn't be any worse than just walking around the campground. And if it's round, it shouldn't be far to an exit anywhere, right?"

Patrice got up. "I need to run into town for a couple of things for my salad for tonight. Anyone need anything?"

Brooke jumped up too. "I'll go with you. I need to pick up a birthday card for my niece."

Patrice looked around the group. Everyone else shook their heads.

"Nope, nothing."

"Me either."

"Thanks for asking."

Patrice and Brooke waved and headed down the road.

Max watched them go and then turned to Buzzy. "You seem to know a lot about the lawsuit. Do you know something about that Lambert Bardsley?" She kept her voice low and tried not to sound accusing.

"I've never met him," Buzzy said.

Max persisted. "But you knew the name."

"Just that he is involved in the lawsuit."

Carole jumped up. "I think we should play some cards. Anyone else up for it?"

Buzzy shook her head. "I have some things I need to take care of before lunch. I'll see you all at the tour." She didn't wait for an answer but headed for her own campsite.

Just Carole, Lil, and Max were left.

Lil cocked her head at Carole. "So, do you really want to play cards, or were you just trying to shut Max up?"

"The latter. What were you trying to do?" she asked Max.

"She knows more than she's telling. She says she saw the list of plaintiffs in this lawsuit against Babs' husband. I just wonder why she was interested enough to know so many of the names."

"Maybe it's just her concern for Babs," Carole said. "Buzzy is a wonderful person who runs a non-profit for autistic adults. I can't imagine her being involved with anything shady."

"You said you've only attended one other event, right?" Max asked.

"Well, two actually. The one Lois took me to, and then one when I got this camper. Why?"

"So you don't know most of these people that well, do you?"

Carole frowned. "Max, these people are my friends. No, I don't know them very well, but they have welcomed me with open arms at a time when I desperately needed it. Please don't start something."

She stood and smoothed her shorts. "I'll fix some sandwiches for lunch." She turned and marched into the camper.

Max sighed. "Don't look at me that way."

"You always have to stir things up," Lil said.

"I didn't start this. Scary things are going on here, and someone needs to get to the bottom of it."

"Playing Sherlock Holmes again. I'll go help Carole."

Max sipped her coffee and looked around the campground. She didn't understand why Carole and Lil were so resistant to getting answers. Babs was a member of the group too and obviously needed help.

Rosie hefted herself to her feet and laid her nose on Max's knee, looking up with soulful eyes. But her gyrating tail gave her away.

"I think maybe we both need a walk, huh, girl?"

Rosie dropped the soulful look and could barely stand still long enough for Max to unhook her tether and attach her leash. They headed down the road to the other loop where there was more activity. She noted again the *For Sale* sign on Lambert Bardsley's fifth wheel. No one was outside there. She wondered if Bardsley knew who

Babs was. Maybe the camper was for sale because of his financial losses. Add him to the suspect list.

Other campsites had adults visiting and children chasing each other. Clouds had moved in and the winds had picked up, but it didn't slow any of the kids down. Max's progress, however, was impeded by the kids who paused in their games long enough to pet Rosie, who enthusiastically received their affections. She had to chuckle at the sight of two men lost in a chat while a scroungy dog grabbed a piece of meat off a grill behind one of the men.

"Hey!" The cook brandished a spatula as he started to chase down the dog. Rosie of course, strained at her leash, eager to aid and abet the thief. Max pulled her back as they continued back to the Glampers' loop.

As they approached the overflow parking, Max saw that Babs' truck had pulled in. Balzac was standing between the truck and the trees talking to someone. Max realized it was Leah. He bent his head toward her in a rather intimate gesture, then squeezed the woman's shoulder before she headed back to the Glamper sites.

Balzac clicked the locks on the truck and was walking toward the road when he spotted Max.

"Hi! Aren't you one of Babs' friends?"

"Yes. I mean, this is my first time with this group. I'm just visiting my sister. But I have chatted with Babs a bit."

"I recognized your dog. You, too, but that's a beautiful dog."

Meaning I'm not beautiful or memorable. "Thank you. She's very special."

Rosie pulled toward Balzac. She always recognized a compliment when she heard one.

"You apparently got Babs' trailer delivered."

"Yeah." Balzac ran his hand through his hair. "I'm afraid their preliminary estimate sounds pretty serious. I hope when they get into it more, the news is better, but that's usually not the case." He paused and looked around. "That woman in your group that everyone calls Buzzy? Do you know her real name?"

Max hesitated. It wasn't a secret. But she wondered why he hadn't asked Leah. Maybe he had a romantic interest? She couldn't see any harm in telling him. "Um, it's Jeanette. Walton, I think. Made me think of the old TV show. My sister said she runs a foundation for autistic adults."

Balzac nodded. "I wondered. She's part of the case against Grayton Grangersmith. He talked her into investing foundation funds with him."

Max swallowed. Not a romantic interest then. No wonder Buzzy knew quite a bit about the lawsuit and who was involved. "I see. Well, thank you for taking the camper to a dealer. I'm sure Babs appreciates it."

"Do you know where she is? I'll give her a report."

"She was going back to Lois' camper to take a pain pill. She might be lying down, but Lois could take a message."

He looked back up the road. "Which one is Lois's camper?"

"I'll show you."

When they got close to Carole's site, Max pointed out the blue and white Shasta. "It looks like they're sitting outside."

"Thanks for your help," Balzac said and continued to the Shasta. Max and Rosie returned to Carole's picnic table. Lil was back outside at the table, her hands wrapped around her coffee mug and her eyes focused on the distance.

Max spoke softly. "I'm not really so far off base as you and Carole think. Owen Balzac just told me that Buzzy is part of that lawsuit against Babs' husband. So she *does* know more than she's saying."

Lil glanced at her sideways and went back to her vacant stare.

"I just mean there are some other things going on here. Maybe they're connected, maybe not. I thought Buzzy was rather rude to Owen because he was part of the lawsuit. But maybe she was worried he was going to spill the beans on her."

Max shook her head and looked around. "This is in confidence, but I want you to understand why I'm concerned. Last night, Leah and I were helping to empty the outside compartments on Babs' camper. In the back we found Leah's phone and fan—everything but the chandelier—that was taken from her earlier."

Lil's head whipped around. "What are you saying?"

"Babs left the campfire early. Maybe someone else put them there, but it raises questions. And just now I saw Leah talking to Owen Balzac, like they know each other well. Maybe *really* well. I just want Carole to be careful who she trusts."

Lil rubbed her forehead. "Did Leah report what she found to the police?"

"Not yet. She said she was too concerned about what Babs had already been through. She hid them at the edge of the woods like the thief had dropped them there. If no one else finds them, she will. But maybe she staged the whole burglary thing." Max shrugged. This going in circles was making her tired.

"Why would she cover up for Babs? Or was she trying to blame Babs?"

"Like I said, she said she didn't want to add to Babs' troubles without evidence. But I don't know what to think any more."

Lil nodded slowly. "I guess I can see why you're suspicious. But Carole has had such a hard time. I hate to see you shoot down her new friendships."

"That's why you and I need to keep our eyes and ears open. I won't confront anyone else—especially if Carole's around. But let me know if you hear anything."

"Okay. Sorry I jumped to conclusions."

Carole came out of the camper bearing a plate of sandwiches. She noticed Max and quickly looked away. "Lil, would you get the plates and napkins, please?"

Max got up. "I will. Lil better save herself for the tour."

"Whatever."

When Max came back out, Carole and Lil were chatting, and Carole seemed more relaxed. Max assumed that Lil had filled Carole in on Max's good intentions.

Carole said, "The hike tomorrow is really supposed to be beautiful but challenging. You have decent hiking shoes?" She looked at Max.

Max grinned. "Yeah. Brought my official Colorado boots."

Carole returned the smile. Max relaxed. She must be forgiven. She began to ask about time of the tour, when shouts erupted across the road.

Carole stood up. "What's going on?"

One word became clearer in the shouts. "Fire!" Max rushed to the road and peered toward the direction of the shouts. The sun was in her eyes, and she wished she had her sunglasses. "It's at Lois' camper!" she yelled back to her sisters before she headed toward the sounds.

CHAPTER SEVEN

MAX HURRIED up the road followed by Carole, with Lil trailing behind. Max reached an angle where she could see the backside of Lois' trailer. Smoke drifted out one of the windows, and women were milling around the scene yelling. Buzzy wielded a fire extinguisher, as Patrice hurried up the road ahead of them carrying another. Carole turned around. "I'll get mine, too," she called to Max and Lil as she ran back to her campsite.

As the sisters rounded the camper to the door side, they found Leah with her hands on Rita's shoulders. Max couldn't tell at first whether she was trying to comfort the woman or shake her. Rita was quivering with sobs. Smoke and rancid smells drifted from the camper but Buzzy's work with the extinguisher appear to have done the trick. Carole returned with her extinguisher and began spraying the area around the window anyway. The screen was torn where someone had tried to reach the fire.

"What happened?" Max asked Leah.

Rita wailed, "I went in to see if Lois was there, and the curtains were on fire! I didn't know what to do!"

Leah shook her head in exasperation. "Buzzy and I came along just then. The fire extinguisher was right inside the door—"

A DNR truck pulled up and a ranger jumped out, almost before it rolled to a stop. He loped over to them and pulled out his phone as he did so. "What's happened?" Without waiting for an answer, he spoke into the phone briefly, and put it back in his pocket.

The ranger turned back to them. His nameplate read Adam Mayers. "Whose camper is this?"

Leah said, "Lois Becker. But I don't think she's here. Rita, did you find her?"

"Noooo." Rita sobbed, not very convincingly.

Buzzy turned to the Ranger Mayers. "She's not in there. I checked. Another woman is staying with her, but neither one is inside."

"Okay, the fire department is coming. Let's get everyone away from here in case the propane tank goes." He reached for Carole's extinguisher. "I'll take over that. Please get your friends away from here."

"C'mon everyone! Down to my place!"

As they headed to Carole's site, they heard a scream behind them and turned to see Lois and Babs returning from the shower house with towels and toiletry bags. Lois had stopped in the middle of the road, her hand covering her mouth as she stared at the bedlam in her site. Leah, Max, and Buzzy hurried toward her as Carole herded the rest toward her camper.

81

"Wha—what is happening?" Lois whispered, standing stock still in the road. Babs simply stared.

Leah took Lois' arm. "There's a fire. Buzzy got it out, I think, but the ranger wants us out of the way, so we're going down to Carole's. We don't know much yet."

Babs put her arm over Lois' shoulders. Her voice was broken as she said, "This is my fault. Whoever is after me knew I was staying with you. I'm so sorry."

Lois shook her head. "It's not your fault. It's the fault of the jerk who's doing these horrible things."

Leah took Lois' arm. "Let's go down to Carole's. That's where everyone is."

Lois reluctantly let Leah guide her as she kept her eyes on her camper. After they passed it, she turned her head several times. By the time they reached Carole's site, they could hear sirens coming down the campground road.

"I don't understand," Lois shook her head after Leah got her seated in a lawn chair and took her towel and shower bag. "We were only gone twenty minutes or so."

"A camper can go up in minutes. It must have just happened," Buzzy said.

Rita spotted an empty chair and didn't notice that Lil was about to sit in. She grabbed it and dragged it into the circle next to Lois. Fortunately, Lil heard the movement behind her and didn't try to sit. She glanced at Max and moved over to the picnic bench next to her sister.

"That Rita is sure a piece of work," Max muttered when Lil got settled.

"Remember that she came up early with Babs last night, too," Lil replied.

Max sat back and looked at Lil. "You mean—"

Lil lowered her voice even more. "She doesn't seem with it enough to even pull it off, but I don't think we can discount that she had the opportunity. She was also the one who 'discovered' the fire."

Max watched Rita chatting away almost dementedly. "Maybe she isn't as scatterbrained as she appears. We need to keep an eye on her."

Carole sat down next to them. "What are you two plotting?"

"Who, us?" Max asked.

Lil pointed back toward Lois' site. "We're just wondering how that started."

"Maybe Lois had a candle burning or something on the stove," Max said.

Carole shook her head. "Not Lois. She's super conscientious."

Max gazed around at the group, and realized that the camaraderie of the night before had dampened. An edginess that had not been present at the taco supper or the campfire had moved in like a light fog. Most of the conversations were muted, punctuated by Rita's dissonant voice.

Leah plopped on the picnic bench across from the sisters. Max moved over next to her. "Have you talked to

Babs about—you know?" she asked in a low voice, although there was so much chatter going on around them, it was unlikely anyone would hear.

"Not yet." She grimaced and chewed her lip, glancing at the noisy group around Lois.

"Lil just pointed out that Rita came up early last night with Babs, and now she was the first one on the fire scene." She looked at Leah, waiting for her reaction.

It wasn't long in coming. "What—? You think *Rita* —?"

Max shrugged. "I don't know anything about her. It's just an odd coincidence. Babs was at the shower with Lois when the fire started. So she obviously didn't start it. And Rita seems like a very odd duck."

"Some would say that about you," Lil told her sister.

Max ignored her. "Do you know her very well?" she asked Leah.

Leah frowned and gazed over to the group in lawn chairs where Rita was interrupting everyone else's comments. "Not really. She doesn't always show up and when she does, she's so flighty, it's hard to get to know her."

"Would she have any reason to target Babs?" Max asked. "It seems obvious these 'accidents' are directed at Babs. She is staying with Lois, after all."

Leah shrugged. "I don't know of any. But there's something else I'm worried about." She paused and looked around at the rest of the group. No one was paying any attention to their conversation.

"What?" Max asked.

"My sister Tammy, who I told you about last night?"

"Yeah?"

"I got a text from her this morning. She said she stopped by last night to see me, but I wasn't at my camper. I don't know how she even knew I was here. Although, I think she follows the Galloping Glampers website. She hardly talks to me, but she keeps close track of a lot of things in my life. Of course, when she stopped, we were down at the campfire."

"What are you thinking?"

"She *could* have taken my stuff and hidden it in Babs' camper. And maybe hung around and later pushed the camper down the hill. She could still be hanging around." Leah nodded toward Lois' camper.

"But why would she have done that? I mean, I could understand why she would take your things, based on what you told us, but why would she target Babs?"

Leah sighed. "I don't know, but I'm worried."

Sophie came running up to the site. Part of her hair was pulled up in a messy bun and the rest swirled around her face. "What happened? I just got back from town when I heard the sirens."

Carole updated her on the events.

"Wow! This is crazy." She spotted the percolator on the table. "Ohhh, coffee! Mind if I grab a cup?"

85

"Go right ahead. Mugs are in that compartment under the table."

Sophie brought her mug over to the picnic table and sat beside Max. Rita let loose with a harsh, screeching laugh. Sophie cringed but didn't make any comment.

"I was told you are a lawyer?" Max said to Sophie.

"Yes. I mean sort of." She grinned. "I'm serving in the state legislature, so I work for a small town firm part time."

"Well, this is just a general question. Several think that all of these 'mishaps'" —she used air quotes— "are related to the trouble Babs' husband got into."

"Certainly no one's come up with anything more likely," Carole added.

Max continued. "But Babs claims she has nothing that anyone can gain from her. Can you think of any reason why she might be a target? Her husband's already being punished, right?"

Sophie turned her mug in her hands. "Yes, he's in prison. But there's also a civil suit."

"I've heard that. Apparently there's quite a large group involved?"

"I believe so."

"Several in this group included, as I understand," Max said.

"Well, that's not surprising. There are quite a few in the group nearing retirement, and Babs has always handed out her husband's business cards. People like to invest with someone they know or have a connection with," Sophie explained.

"Is Babs named in the suit, do you know?" Lil asked.

"No, I don't."

Max persisted. "But even if she is, she says she doesn't have anything but her camper and old truck. Why would anyone go after her?"

Sophie shook her head. "Unless—", she looked around the site and was apparently satisfied that only the group at the table was listening. "No, it's too crazy."

"What?" Carole asked.

"It's possible—if she has a sizable insurance policy—I suppose someone might be trying to add that to her husband's assets. But how would one of the plaintiffs in the suit even know about a policy?"

She rotated her mug again. "I think it's more likely that it's a revenge issue—*if*, and it's a big *if*—these incidents have anything to do with her husband's crimes, rather than someone trying to do away with her. I need more coffee." She got up and went to the coffee pot.

The sisters looked at each other. Carole's eyes were wide. "That's just too gruesome."

Lil patted her hand. "It seems to me that most of these 'accidents' have been intended to harm and to cause fear, but none were really deadly."

"They could have been," Carole said.

"Yes, they could have, but we don't know that was the intention. The person who rolled the camper could see the trees, and wouldn't expect the camper to gain much speed in that distance. When they set the fire, they may have known that Babs and Lois were at the shower."

Sophie returned to the table. Lil repeated her theory about the incidents.

Sophie nodded. "Like I said, I think revenge is the most likely motive. And I agree with you about the likelihood that these incidents were intended as nonfatal pranks."

Carole sighed. "I just can't imagine anyone in this group being that cruel. I mean, even if they weren't trying to kill her. There's some strong and a few rather strange personalities, but they've always been so supportive."

Lil got up from the table. "I need to do some walking. Doctor's orders. Max, you want to be my nursemaid?"

Max started to protest but caught a look in Lil's eye that indicated this was more than a walk. "I suppose. C'mon, Rosie. It's your lucky day."

"I think I'll take my cane, just to be on the safe side." Lil went to collect it while Max hooked up Rosie's leash.

"Which way do you want to go?" Max asked.

"Let's walk up toward the entrance and see where this hike tomorrow is going to go."

When they had put some distance between them and Carole's campsite, Max said, "So what's up?"

"I just wanted to talk about this situation without worrying about who's listening."

As if to confirm this statement, Rita's screeching laugh floated up to them on the breeze.

Max raised her eyebrows. "I thought *I* was the one trying to stir things up."

"Yeah. Well." Lil looked up at her sister from under her bangs and leaned on her cane. "First, this group is so important to Carole. But I would feel better about the time she spends with them if we get to the bottom of what's happening here. If not, I'd worry about her every time she goes on one of these weekends, wouldn't you?"

"You're right. But, it was only a couple of hours ago that you thought I was trying to ruin her relationships with this group."

Lil sighed. "I know. But you explained your concerns and I accepted them. And then the fire occurred. So give it a rest. There's a good chance you're right—is that what you want to hear?"

Max gave her a smirk and put her arm around her sister's shoulders. "You got it."

Lil stumbled slightly. "Well. Don't knock me down! I won't forgive you for that."

Max said, "Oops, I'm sorry!" as she helped Lil regain her balance. "Do you have any new thoughts as to what's going on?"

"Just questions. Who do you think might be behind this?"

They came around the curve and saw the sign for the waterfall. "There's a bench up there by the entrance to the boardwalk," Max said. "Are you ready to sit for a few minutes?"

"Yes. Very ready."

Chapter Eight

THE BENCH SAT on a platform which began the downhill ramp. The waterfall wasn't visible, but the late morning sun made a pleasant vista through the trees. Lil lowered herself gingerly using her cane and drew in a deep breath.

"That's far enough. It should make my doctor — and my muscles — happy. So bring me up to date on who you think the suspects are."

"This is not a definitive list, so if you have any additions — or subtractions — I know I can trust you to pipe up. First is Owen Balzac. He seems on the surface to be very helpful to Babs, and she is convinced of that. But he's part of the lawsuit — in fact, if we dug deep, I wouldn't be surprised if he was the instigator."

"People do have a right to try and get money back when they've been scammed," Lil protested.

"Absolutely. Maybe instigator is the wrong word. But he would be in a position to know what redress is possible and to encourage clients to join in."

"True. And based on what Sophie told us, he might be the most likely one to know what Babs' life insurance situation is, since he and her husband were partners."

"Good point. And as far as we know, he had means and opportunity. But, we don't actually *know* where he was last night. And really don't have any way of finding out."

"Also true. Who else do you think?"

"Maybe Buzzy since she is part of the lawsuit too? The thing is, pretty much everyone had opportunity to push that camper down the hill so that doesn't narrow it down. Buzzy seems like a really good person, but apparently she invested funds from her non-profit. The work they do or even her job could be in jeopardy if there were big losses. She was one of the first on the scene at the fire."

Lil shook her head. "She was the one who put it out!"

"Could have been just to deflect suspicion. Everything is so fuzzy. Finding those stolen items in Babs' camper, for example. How does that compute? Did Babs take them, or Leah put them there to throw blame on Babs for some reason? What seems more likely is Leah's sister Tammy — you know, she mentioned her last night." Max went on to tell Lil about the message Leah had gotten from Tammy that morning. "It sounds like a very contentious relationship."

Lil nodded. "Leah mentioned her and her problems when we first looked at her camper yesterday."

"Yes, and don't forget Rita. She had the opportunity to take the stuff from Leah and supposedly discovered the fire. She *could* also be involved in the lawsuit."

Max leaned back on the bench and swatted at a fly. "I just can't see her as being organized enough to plan these events. Actually, we have no idea how many or who in the group invested with Babs' husband. Or are involved with the lawsuit."

Lil nodded. "We really don't know much for sure." She looked down the walk as far as they could see on the trail. "I think I should be able to do this tomorrow."

"Sure. And if you want to turn back, that's fine with me. We'll just play it by ear."

Lil stood. "I guess we have to play this mystery by ear, too." They headed back to the campsite.

BY THE TIME THEY GOT SEATED again at Carole's picnic table, the group had grown to include all of the Glampers present. Ranger Mayers walked up to the group a few minutes later.

"Who is the owner of that camper?" he asked, looking around.

Lois raised her hand. "I am. Lois Becker."

"It's safe to go back there, now. The firemen say it's not safe to stay in it—partly because of chemicals

93

possibly released by the heat. But I'm sure you're anxious to check it out and get your things."

Lois wrung her hands. "Thank you. I understand. What could have caused it, do you know?"

Mayers removed his cap and scratched his head. "It looks like a candle that was left burning on the table caught the curtains on fire."

"What? A candle? I've never burned any candles in that camper. I know what a danger they are. I don't even keep any in there." She looked wildly around the group. "Did anyone—? No, of course not."

Buzzy spoke up. "The screen by that table was ripped or cut before I started spraying through there with the fire extinguisher."

The ranger looked surprised. "You didn't do that?"

Buzzy shook her head. "No, sir."

He took a pad and pen from his shirt pocket. "I'd better get some notes here. What is your name and site number, ma'am?"

"Jeanette Walton. Site 16."

"It sounds like you think the fire was set. Is that the case?"

Several around the circle nodded. Rita, of course, couldn't just nod. "I found it! I went in looking for Lois and the curtains were on fire. No one was in there."

The ranger blinked. "Why did you go in? Did you know there was a fire?"

"I knocked and no one answered."

Mayers frowned but wisely decided to forego any further exploration of Rita's actions. He turned to Lois. "Under the circumstances, I'm going to ask you to wait on going back into your camper. I need to turn this information over to the fire department and the police. Do you have somewhere you can go?"

Patrice said, "We'll take care of her — and Babs."

Others nodded and volunteered space.

Leah asked, "Can someone go in and close the window so Lois doesn't have any wildlife visitors?"

"Ms. Becker, how about if you go in with me, and you can get any personal items you need, we'll close the window and lock it up?"

Lois heaved herself out of her chair. "Thank you. That's really kind of you."

Babs walked along with them toward Lois' camper.

Watching them go, Buzzy said, "If this keeps up, all of us will be staying in one camper. It won't be pretty." There were a few chuckles, but the statement was too close to the truth to be taken too lightly.

"Seriously, I have an extra bed in my camper," Patrice said.

"I do too," Jessi said. "Babs could stay with me and that way I could keep an eye on her medical condition."

"Well. I sure don't have room." Rita looked around the group and let loose her shrill laugh. "I barely have room for me."

"Of course," Leah mumbled out the side of her mouth to Max.

The ranger, Lois, and Babs were back about ten minutes later. The women each carried a small plastic grocery sack. The ranger promised to get back to them as soon as he knew something.

After he walked away, Buzzy turned to the rest of the group. "Well. What do you think? Should we still do the barn tour?"

Jessi said, "I think we're safer in the barn than in this campground."

Buzzy looked at Lois and Babs. "What about you ladies? You've had the most stressful morning."

Lois shrugged and looked at Babs. "I'm fine with it," Babs said. "Need something to take my mind off what's been going on here."

THEY ARRANGED CAR POOLS to transport everyone to the round barn. Carole, Leah and Lil rode in Max's car.

"This is so cool," Leah said as she folded her legs into the back seat. "Have you had it long?"

"About eight years."

"It's really fun to travel in," Lil said. "We've been all over in it."

"Usually causing trouble," Carole added.

The barn sat back from the road in an open field that included a large parking lot. The red paint and white trim appeared fresh and crisp. The barn was perched on a limestone base with four-pane white windows evenly spaced around that level. The ground sloped around to the back exposing the whole level on that side. A cement ramp led up to double doors in the front, which were slid to each side to provide a welcoming entrance. The huge domed roof was topped by a small cupola.

They trooped up the ramp and into the cool interior. A large, jovial man in a flannel shirt, bib overalls, and a ruddy complexion sat at a table with a milk can for donations and stacks of fliers.

"Welcome! Is this your first trip to the round barn?"

Most of them nodded.

"Well, you're in for a treat!" He pointed to a round structure in the center. "That's the silo and it was built first, so it helps to support the roof. It's eighty feet tall. Now you'll hear of barns that are bigger but not really round. Usually six- or eight-sided. You can wait for a guided tour or take the self guided version. There are cards to read all along the way."

"I think I'm up for the self-guided tour," Buzzy said. The rest of the group agreed. They picked up flyers and started around the main floor. About halfway up, a floor covered about two-thirds of the barn and formed the upper level, which had been used as a hay mow. The barn was clean and well-kept, but still held an earthy smell. Antique farm equipment—everything from cream separators to corn shellers—was displayed with explanations, dates, and names of donors.

"These are great to see," Lois said. "I remember a lot of these things from my grandpa's farm."

Babs nodded. "Owen said this would be well worth our time. He volunteers here sometimes."

When they finished the first floor, they were directed out a side door and down a ramp to a door in the exposed basement. Inside, stanchions creating tie stalls for the original owner's Black Angus cattle formed a circle around the bottom of the silo. Inside the circle was a manger that could be filled with the feed.

Buzzy read the explanation posted by the door. "That silo goes up through the whole barn and allowed the farmer to fill it with hay or chopped corn from the mow upstairs and pull it out here to fill the manger."

"Ingenious," Max said.

"What is *this*?" Rita asked. She pointed to a large metal bin suspended by chains from a track in the ceiling that ran around the outside walkway behind the cattle stalls. It had a U-shaped bottom and was about two by four feet.

Lil giggled as she read from her flyer. "It's a manure bucket. The workers could pull it around and clean up behind the cows."

"Ewww. A giant pooper-scooper?" Rita said.

"It didn't do the scooping—the workers had to do that."

"Sounds like a fun job."

They wandered around the lower level, marveling at the technology developed a century ago to make cattle raising as efficient as possible.

As they headed back up the ramp to the main entrance, Max asked, "So what's for supper? Steak? Black Angus, perhaps?"

"Almost as good," Carole said. "Stone soup."

Max laughed. "You mean—?"

"Yup. We've all been assigned to bring a veggie, meat, tomato sauce, broth or some herbs and cheese. We'll throw it all in one pot."

"Is there a pizza delivery place nearby if that doesn't turn out?"

"Skeptic."

They drove back to the campground and decided, in view of the long night and morning, some naps were in order. Carole and Lil took the beds in the camper, and, after a short walk for Rosie, Max opted for her ebook and a chaise lounge out under the trees. Rosie collapsed with her head under the chaise as if it would hide her from everyone. It was a beautiful early fall afternoon. A few lazy bugs hovered in the area but didn't land. Before long, Max's book dropped in her lap, and her head lolled to the side.

She jolted awake to a low growl coming from under the chaise. Rosie extracted herself and took a guard stance. Max sat up and squinted at a shadow looming at the edge of the campsite.

99

"Oh! I'm sorry to wake you. I thought you were reading." Lambert Bardsley stood there looking extremely uncomfortable.

Max smiled. "I was, but a nap won out. Can I help you with something?"

"I was just wondering. Your friend, who had the camper accident last night—is she by any chance Grayton Grangersmith's wife?"

Max hesitated. Was it any of his business? She didn't want to be responsible for any more 'accidents.' "I'm just a visitor to this group. Carole—" she nodded toward the trailer, "—is my sister. Why do you ask?"

Bardsley shifted from one foot to the other and looked around. "That guy has caused me a lot of grief. He's ruined my bank account, and maybe even my marriage."

Max didn't know what to say. Finally, she said, "I'm sorry to hear that."

He rubbed a hand over his partially bald head. "Yeah, well, it is what it is. I just wondered, y'know? Thanks." He turned and walked away.

As Max sat up in her chair, absently petting Rosie and trying to make sense of the visit, Carole opened the door of the camper, and stepped out, stretching her arms.

"That felt great! Who was that?" She motioned at the figure of Bardsley walking down the road.

"Lambert Bardsley. The guy from the other loop who was helping out last night. He wanted to know if Babs was Grayton Grangersmith's wife. Said

Grangersmith ruined his bank account and maybe his marriage. We heard he and his wife arguing yesterday when we walked down through that loop, remember?"

"So maybe another suspect in all of this mess?" Carole said.

"I wondered about that earlier, but apparently he didn't know who Babs is until after last night."

"He says."

"But why would he ask if he already knew? It would just raise suspicion."

Carole thought a moment. "You're right." She looked at her watch. "We'd better get ready for supper."

"What are you contributing to the soup?"

"I have some tomato sauce and parmesan cheese. And there's brownies left from last night. Not for the soup, of course. I'll see if Lil is awake."

THE SUPPER GATHERING was at Sophie's camper, a small popup. Sophie was stirring a large cast iron kettle over the fire. Carole added her tomato sauce to the mix and admired the colorful concoction. Max put the leftover brownies on the dessert table where Buzzy was arranging the offerings.

Buzzy looked at her watch. "We've had five or six hours now with no disasters. Could we be lucky enough that that's the end of it?"

"It depends on what the culprit was trying to achieve. If it was just to scare someone, or maybe all of us, they could be done. On the other hand…"

Lil hobbled over, relying on her cane more than usual. "What are you two plotting?"

"Just wondering if things have quieted down for good or we should be waiting for another shoe to drop," Max said.

But they began to relax over bowls of soup, relish trays, and loaves of crusty bread.

Brooke was looking at her phone. "Looks like we might get some rain tomorrow afternoon. Maybe we should have done the hike today and the barn tour tomorrow."

Buzzy shook her head. "The barn isn't open tomorrow."

"Good reason," Brooke said.

"Do we want a campfire tonight?" Sophie asked the group. "I have firewood ready."

"I think Babs needs the rest, and I expect most of us do. It was a short night. I'm in favor of turning in early," said Jessi.

Buzzy threw up her hands. "Doctor's orders! What can we do?"

It was a quiet night in the Glampers' end of the campground.

CHAPTER NINE

THE NEXT MORNING, the group gathered at Buzzy's camper before the walk. Most carried water bottles and walking sticks.

Buzzy signaled for attention. "The entrance to the waterfall walk is along the road that comes into the campground — only about 200 feet back. The boardwalk goes downhill but very gently." She glanced reassuringly at Lil.

Lois waved her hands. "No problem. There is a board walk most of the way down to the river. The hike up to the falls might not be doable. But she could use a walker if she needs it on the first part."

Lil shook her head. "No, I've progressed beyond that. And we looked at it yesterday. But I'll probably be pretty slow. I wouldn't want to hold anyone up."

"Don't worry about that," Buzzy said. "This group has all different levels of physical ability. We're usually strung out for about a half mile on any walk."

"Or we're just strung out, period." Lois threw back her head and laughed.

Buzzy continued. "When we get to the waterfall, there is a path leading up to the top, but it's pretty challenging. Those who want to climb it, can do so, and the rest of us will wait at the bottom or head back. Everyone ready?"

Lois turned to Babs. "Are you sure you feel up to this? I'd be glad to stay back with you."

"No way. I'm fine. If I don't go, they'll talk about me." Babs grinned.

The others laughed and Patrice said "At least when you get lost, with that shirt on, you'll be easy to find" She pointed at the safety orange hoodie that Babs was wearing.

Babs pirouetted. "Most of my clothes are still in the camper. Lois lent me this."

"And now most of *my* clothes smell like smoke," Lois said, a little ruefully.

Buzzy put her finger alongside her cheek. "Maybe when we get back from the walk, we need to find a thrift shop and do a little shopping."

Everyone cheered.

Buzzy led them out along the road. The entrance to the boardwalk was marked by a sign that said *Raccoon Falls* with a hiker image.

"I hope the name doesn't mean there will be little bandits along the way trying to grab our water bottles," Jessie said.

Rita stopped. "I forgot a water bottle! I'd better go back."

Leah sighed. "I have an extra in my backpack."

"Oh, thank you. That would be great."

That hurdle surmounted, the women continued on. The boardwalk consisted of eight or ten foot flat sections broken up by flights of three to five steps so it was an easy descent. A sturdy railing ran along the downhill side. Rosie pulled at her leash, eager to explore the woods and meet the natives. The red of the sumac clumps and yellow of the silver maples promised a riot of color in the woods later in the season. The boardwalk was covered in places with carpets of leaves that rivaled the rugs in Becky's camper.

"What a gorgeous day!" Babs said, loud enough to carry back to Max, Lil, and Carole, who brought up the end of the line. Max marveled at her spirit after the night and day she had. But then there was the question of the stolen items in her camper. Could Babs have pulled the chocks herself and rolled the camper? She could have then caused the injury to her head to give herself an alibi. Another possible suspect.

She thought about seeing Leah the morning before with Owen Balzac. She could have taken her own items from her camper and hidden them in Babs's the night before. She led Max right to the stolen items when they emptied the camper. There were just too many possibilities.

As they approached the bottom of the boardwalk, the sound of the waterfall increased. Flies looking for warmth buzzed around them. The steps ended on a rocky point jutting out just past the pool made by the falls. The falls were not wide—just a narrow cascade tumbling down the middle of a horseshoe cliff. The woods around created a peaceful and colorful glen highlighted with spots of sunlight. As they looked downstream from the waterfall they could see the glint of the lake through the trees.

Brooke drew in a deep breath. "This is awesome! Who knew something like this would be in the middle of this park? Max, Carole, and Lil! How about if I snap your picture with the falls in the background?"

"That would be great," Carole said and handed her phone to Brooke. The three sisters posed with Lil perched on a large boulder and Max and Carole behind her.

Just as Brooke said, "Say cheese," Max felt a push against her left side.

"Oops! Sorry! " Rita righted herself and waved her phone around. "I was just trying to get a selfie."

Max started to rebuke her, but Brooke said, "Wait 'til I get done with this one, and I'll take one of you so you don't fall in the river."

"Oh, good idea," Rita laughed. "Thank you!"

Buzzy said, "The path to the top is over there in those trees." She pointed at a sign with the familiar hiker icon. "It's pretty steep."

"It doesn't look too bad," Lois said.

"It isn't at first. But around that first bend, it changes. You want sturdy shoes and a hiking stick, like I said this morning."

Max turned to Lil. "You are definitely not going. Rosie and I can stay with you."

Leah said, "I think I'm going to wait down here, too." She turned to Lil. "Can you stand a little company?"

"Certainly!" and to Max, she said, "You aren't the boss of me. But I had already decided not to try it. This will be a lovely place to hang out and we don't need you. Right, Rosie?" She turned back to Max. "Are you sure *you're* up to it?"

To Lil's surprise, Max paused and looked up at the falls again before replying. "I think I can make it. If not, I'll just turn around and come back down."

The rest started up the first grade, a gentle slope. The path was wide, but surfaced with large gravel that was difficult to walk on. Much of it had washed away, and a large rut down the middle required constant vigilance to avoid twisting an ankle. Suddenly the slope got steeper, and Max found herself relying on her hiking stick for almost every step.

Jessi was behind her, with Sophie following. "You doing okay, Max?"

"Yes, but I'm pretty slow. Would you like to go around me?"

"No, no. I'm fine. Just checking."

Max started to make defensive comment about her age, but then thought that since she was old enough to be Jessi's grandmother, Jessi was just voicing concern.

"Thank you," she said instead.

107

"I think you are doing amazingly well," Jessi continued. "Do you hike a lot?"

"Not daily, but when I can. Colorado has some beautiful places to walk." Max realized she was huffing a little and decided to stick to shorter sentences. Rita yelped behind them.

"You okay?" Jessi called back.

"Yeah, but my right foot is hurting. I think my shoe's too small. I'm going to go back," Rita yelled.

"Okay!"

"Lil will be thrilled," Max commented to Sophie.

Sophie grinned. "I'm sure."

Crashing sounds came from their right.

"*What* is that?" Jessi asked. "I hope a deer. We don't often have bears around here."

More thrashing was followed by laughter and shouts. Max stopped to catch her breath and caught sight of a couple of figures through the trees down in the ravine. "Worse than bears. Teenagers, I think."

Jessi caught up to her. "You're right. Apparently they didn't want to take the path."

The sounds continued as they went up the hill. Max sighed. "That energy is just wasted on kids that age. Now *I* could *do* something with that." She used her walking stick to keep her balance while she stepped across the center rut to what looked like more solid footing.

She still twisted her ankle slightly. "Oooh!"

Jessi grabbed her elbow. "Are you okay?"

"Yeah, it's more my natural reaction anytime I think I *might* fall." She tested the ankle and was satisfied that nothing was sprained or broken. She continued the climb. They caught up with Babs.

"How are you doing?" Max asked her.

"Just fine. I'm trying not to move too fast."

"Good. That's what I need to do."

They continued to hear shouts and giggles from the woods. As the trail continued up the hill, the land began to fall off to the right on the side away from the waterfall. Birch trees, sumac, and spindly pines blocked the view of the bottom. The voices moved down into the ravine. Shouts that sounded like challenges and catcalls echoed through the trees.

"So much for the peacefulness of nature," Max said to Babs. They reached a level area with a rustic log bench that overlooked the ravine.

"I'm ready for a break," Max said. She turned to Babs. "How about you?" She wasn't really tired but figured the other woman might need some encouragement to rest.

"That's a great idea," Sophie said. "It's a beautiful spot."

They seated themselves and Max rubbed her back a little for effect. Jessi walked to the edge of the ravine and leaned on a big silver maple.

"How much farther to the top, do you know?" Max asked Jessi.

"Yes, I've hiked this before. We're about halfway."

109

Babs looked up, surprised. "That's all?"

Jessi nodded.

"Whoa. Now that I'm sitting, I don't know if I have enough energy to go that far." Babs leaned back on the bench. "I think I'll just wait here for you to come back down."

"I can go back down with you, if you want," Jessi offered.

"Certainly not. You go on up." Babs waved her off.

"If you don't mind, I'll wait with you," Max said. "I twisted my ankle back there when we started, and I think I might be pushing my luck to keep going. Besides, we agreed this morning, no one should be alone."

"Sure. Welcome the company."

Jessi shook a finger at them. "Now you two behave yourselves, and don't go running off with those crazy teenagers and getting them in trouble."

Babs folded her hands in her lap and put on an angelic face. "Yes, ma'am."

"Bring back some good photos," Max said, and Sophie brandished her camera.

"Sophie was right; it is a beautiful spot," Max said.

"And it feels so good to just sit. I love the Glampers, but yesterday it seemed like everyone was talking more and louder than usual."

"That could be because of your head injury."

Babs nodded. "Could be."

They sat in silence for a few minutes. Max pointed out an oriole in one of the pines, and they smiled at an outburst from one of the kids in the ravine.

Babs shifted a bit on the bench and then cleared her throat. "Um, Leah said you were with her Friday night when she found her stolen items in my camper?"

Max had just been trying to figure out a way to broach the subject. She hadn't been sure if Leah had had a chance to talk to Babs since she asked her. Obviously she had.

"Yes, I was." Max decided to leave it wide open for Babs to explain, rather than ask questions.

"I didn't take them! Honest! But I did hear something after I went to bed. It could have been a storage door closing."

"Was it before you went to sleep or did it wake you up?"

Babs rubbed her forehead. "I'm not sure. I think I was partially asleep. You know when you're kind of in no man's land."

"I was just wondering if someone could have put those items in the compartment and then pulled the chocks and pushed your camper down the hill?"

"I don't know. It seemed like there was time in between, but I really have no idea."

Max leaned back on the bench. "It's very puzzling. My sister Lil pointed out yesterday that so far none of these incidents have been deadly—I mean they could have been, but your trailer didn't roll very far, and you and Lois were at the showers when the fire was set. Perhaps the culprit knew that and is just trying to frighten you?"

Babs was silent for a bit. "I never thought about that, but maybe you're right." She put her head in her hands. "I'm really scared, so if someone is trying to frighten me, it's working."

Max put her hand on Babs' back. "I'm sorry. I didn't mean to upset you. It won't help your headache either."

Babs sat up straight again. Max was reminded of the change in her demeanor when she and Lil first saw the woman the day before.

"I should just go home. I'm afraid I'm a danger to everyone. But at home I would be alone, and I'm afraid of that too." She looked at Max. "What should I do?"

Being a firstborn, Max was used to issuing orders and advice, but at Babs' question, she froze up. If she encouraged her to stay, and anything did happen to anyone in the campground, she would never forgive herself. On the other hand, Babs could be right about the risks of being home alone, too.

"I don't know. I wish I did, but you're right. It's hard to say which is more dangerous."

"But if I go home, at least I'm not putting anyone else at risk."

"That's assuming what's happened is directed at you," Max said. "Someone else could be the target, or it might just be random acts by a bunch of kids." She

112

nodded over her shoulder at the laughter and the shouts coming from the ravine.

"That doesn't seem likely, under the circumstances," Babs said.

Maxine couldn't disagree. Just then her phone rang.

It was Lil. "Hi! How's it going?"

"Fine. Babs and I decided halfway was good enough for us, so we're resting on a bench at a great spot along the trail. How are you doing?"

There was a short pause. "Fine, I guess. Actually, I'm getting pretty tired and I'm thinking about going back to Carole's camper and laying down. I have my cane. It shouldn't be a problem."

Max was torn. "Just a minute. Let me talk to Babs and I'll call you right back." She didn't wait for a response but hung up and turned to Babs. "That was my sister. You know she had a knee replacement recently, and she's getting uncomfortable. But I don't want her going back to the campground alone—she tends to take risks that she shouldn't."

Babs waved her off. "Go ahead. I'll be fine."

"Leah and Rita are both down there, I think. I'll have one of them come up. You shouldn't be alone."

"Leah, I hope," Babs said with an impish grin, "but either one would be fine."

Max nodded and called Lil back. "Wait until I get down there. Could you have Leah come up to sit with Babs?"

113

"Leah went back to the campground. Rita's here. She could probably go back with me, if you don't trust me." Lil chuckled.

"Um, have her come up here. I'll be down in a few minutes." She hung up and turned to Babs. "Sorry to tell you, but Rita is coming. Leah has already gone back."

"Go ahead and go. I'm sure I'll be fine for five or ten minutes."

Max hesitated. "Are you sure it's okay?"

"Get! or I'll sic Rita on you!"

Max laughed and grabbed her hiking stick. "I'll be back."

"Now you're the terminator?"

Max could hear Babs chuckling as she picked her way back down the path. She didn't meet Rita until she was almost back at the bottom. Rita hobbled along with only the toe of her right foot in her shoe with her heel hanging over the back.

"This shoe doesn't fit," she said when she noticed Max eyeing her foot.

"I'm sorry. I guess you said that earlier. Thanks for coming up to stay with Babs. I just don't think she should be alone," Max said. But she wondered how much help Rita would be if there was trouble.

Lil was standing on the bottom platform doing a few stretches and exercises. She looked up as Max came down the path. "I really don't need a babysitter."

"Maybe not, but why take a chance? Besides, there's too much crazy stuff going on around here that I'm not sure anyone should be out alone."

"Yeah, yeah, yeah." Using her cane, Lil started up the first set of stairs, stepping both feet on each tread and helping herself along with her cane. Max followed along behind her, one hand holding Rosie's leash and the other on Lil's back in case she would lose her balance. She sensed that Lil wanted to comment that it was unnecessary, but was holding her tongue. They made their way slowly up the stairs. In the last stretch of steps, Lil tripped and nearly went down, but Max caught her.

Lil gave a grateful but rueful smile. "I guess you're right. I shouldn't be out alone. I was doing so well at home."

"This place is quite different than your home, in case you hadn't noticed."

"Right."

When they got to Carole's camper, Max helped Lil up the steps. Lil kicked off her shoes and laid down on the couch.

"Don't get too comfortable," Max said. "I'm leaving Rosie here, and I want you to lock the door after I leave. And you have your phone?"

"Of course. I'll be fine." Lil smiled and waved her sister off.

CHAPTER TEN

BY THE TIME MAX RETURNED to the boardwalk and descended the steps again, her ankle was starting to really bother her—she didn't have to fake it. As she got close to the bottom, she heard crying.

Rita sat on a large rock sobbing and Jessi stood behind her, rubbing her shoulders. Sophie stood to the side, and looked up at the trees.

"What's the matter?" Max asked.

Jessi started to speak, but Rita blurted out, "Babs is gone!"

Max frowned. "What do you mean, gone?"

"When I got up to the bench, she wasn't there."

"And you didn't meet her on the way up?"

"No—no. I'm sorry."

"There's nothing to be sorry for. She must have decided to try and make it to the top, but I wish she would have waited," Max said.

Jessi was shaking her head. "No, we came back from the top and found Rita at the bench but no Babs. We would have run into her if she continued the hike."

"Okay." Max rubbed her head. "This is really concerning, then. Given Babs' condition and the threats against her, we've got to find her. Are the rest still up at the top, Jessi?" Before Jessi could respond, Max turned to Rita, who had resumed her crying. "Rita, I know you're upset, but that won't help. We have to get a search started and we'll need *every*one's help." She turned back to Jessi and Sophie. "Are they all up there?"

Jessi looked surprised and glanced sideways at Rita, but said, "I think so."

"Since you're more spry, please go back up to the top and get the rest to help, would you?"

Jessi said, "Sure. Do you have your phone?"

Max pulled it out of her pocket and handed it to her. "Put your number in there and I'll do the same for you."

Jessi pulled out her own phone, swiped up a couple of screens, and handed it to Max. They traded the phones back. Jessi and Sophie started up the hill with long strides.

Max said, "Rita, why don't we go back up the path and search as much as we can see along both sides. She has that bright orange shirt on so should be easy to spot."

She dialed Lil and filled her in on what was going on. "I know you need to rest but could you go up to the host's spot and have them get hold of one of the rangers? They need to start a search."

"Sure. I want to help. I feel so useless."

"Yeah, yeah," Max said.

Lil snorted. "I didn't expect gratitude. Let you know what I find out."

"Thanks."

Max turned to Rita, who was sniffing and drying her tears. Holding back her exasperation with this woman, she said, "Let's start up the trail and see what we can find. Will you be okay?"

Rita nodded and stuffed a wadded tissue in her pocket. Max led the way, moving slowly so as not to aggravate her sore ankle and choosing her route carefully aided by her walking stick.

"Why don't you watch the left side of the trail and I'll watch the right so we don't miss anything?"

Rita's "Okay" was muffled.

The morning sun was angling through the trees from the east, creating dark pockets in some areas. But clouds were moving in from the west and the search would become more difficult as the sky darkened. Max felt a need to hurry, but knew that wouldn't be wise or thorough. They could still hear distant shouts and laughter from the teenagers.

"Someone will need to check with those kids. Maybe they saw or heard something. Did you ever see them or which way they were going?"

Rita slapped her arm. "The mosquitos are getting bad. I saw two boys I think—it's hard to tell anymore—and it looked like they were climbing the other side of the ravine."

Max was relieved that the whine seemed to have gone out of Rita's voice. "That would take them back to the road, I think. It sounds like they're still in the woods."

118

"They might not be staying together," Rita pointed out.

"True. Stop a minute. Look at these branches. It looks like someone has gone down into the ravine from here. See the broken ones?"

"Should we go down there and check?"

Max hesitated. "I don't know. I feel like we should at least go up as far as the bench, first." She pointed at the broken branches. "This could have happened days ago. What do you think?"

Rita peered down the hillside. "Now that you say that, this doesn't look real fresh. Maybe we could mark it and see what else we find?"

"Good idea. Do you have anything—" Max was rummaging in the pockets of her windbreaker. "Wait a minute." She pulled out Rosie's leash. "This will work. I'll just have to remember to get it on the way down. It's her favorite." She looped the leash around a tree beside the possible trail.

"How do you know that?"

Max chuckled. "I'm kidding. Anything that allows her to go for a walk is okay with her."

They continued the climb, reaching the place where the ruts made it more difficult.

"I'm afraid I'll have to slow down even more here."

"Do you want to lean on me?" Rita asked.

Her question took Max by surprise. It was the first offer she had heard from Rita to help someone else.

"Thank you, I think I can manage with my stick. But I appreciate the offer, and I'll let you know if I need help. Let's keep on."

Rita was right; the mosquitos were getting worse. "You don't have any bug repellent with you, do you?"

Rita shook her head as she swatted another pest on her neck. "I'm afraid not. I think Jessi has some."

"We'll hope so." They trudged on up the trail. Max stopped again to listen. "I think I hear a siren in the distance. Maybe the cavalry is arriving."

"The cavalry? What do you mean?"

It was becoming clear to Max that Rita took everything literally. "The Sheriff. Bringing proper searchers, I hope."

"Oh. Right."

They reached the little clearing with the bench. Max examined the area around the bench for any clues to Babs' disappearance.

"I see something!" Rita said excitedly, pointing behind the bench. An orange plastic water bottle lay partially hidden by a tangle of weeds a couple of feet down the slope.

"That's the one Babs was carrying, I'm sure!" Max said. She started to sidestep down the hillside, but Rita grabbed her arm.

"Wait! I'll get it. You shouldn't try that."

Max stepped back, again startled by Rita's change in demeanor. Rita pulled a couple of elderberry bush branches back, and started to reach for the bottle. She glanced down the hill and stopped. "There's a path here down into that ravine!"

"Don't slip," Max warned, thinking of Rita's earlier clumsiness. "Here, take my hand."

Rita did and managed to reach the bottle. Max helped her back up and took the bottle. "This is definitely the one Babs had. It has her name on it and still has water in it."

Rita pulled back the branches again so that Max could see the path. "Do you suppose Babs went this way?"

"I don't believe she would have done that voluntarily. If she went that way, I bet someone forced her."

They could hear the voices of the teenagers closer now and they seemed right below them.

Max peered down into the ravine. "I think we should try that path and see if we can talk to those kids."

Rita's eyes widened. "Are you sure? It looks awfully steep."

"We won't know until we try it. We can come back if it's too bad."

"I hope so," Rita muttered. "Let me go first." She pulled the branches back again and started down.

Max took careful sidesteps, aided by her walking stick, and watching for roots and rocks that could trip her up. About five feet down, the trail turned to the side and was more level for a short distance. They still needed to watch their footing as well as trying to avoid getting slapped in the face by branches. Rita turned back frequently to check on Max's progress.

"Still upright," Max assured her. "This isn't too bad so far."

"So far," Rita agreed. "I just wish we could see farther ahead." The low hanging branches not only impeded their progress, but also obscured the route down the hill.

"One step at a time. Does it look to you like anyone's been down this trail recently?"

Rita turned around and looked up the hill. "No, but it doesn't look like we have either."

"Good point."

Every five to ten feet the trail would turn and head downhill and then level out again, like a hairpin mountain road on a much smaller scale. They reached a pile of boulders and fallen trees, where they encountered the owners of the voices they had been hearing. Three or four young teenage boys and two girls were climbing on the rocks and balancing on the logs. They were making so much noise that they didn't notice Max and Rita until they were a few feet away.

One lanky boy with a bright orange mullet, a pierced ear and a black tee shirt festooned with glowing skulls stood and pointed.

"Whoa! We got company! Race, I think your girlfriend's here." He put his hands on his hips, threw back his head, and laughed.

Another boy, incredibly handsome with piercing blue eyes and black curly hair cut in a fade, peeked up from the other side of a boulder. His face fell in disappointment, and he yelled "Very funny, Jason!"

Max had never had children and had always taught college level, so she found it almost unbelievable that most kids this age actually turned into reasonable, thinking young adults a few years later.

One of the girls, a blond, called out, "Grow up you guys." And to Rita and Maxine, "I'm sorry. Don't pay any attention to them."

Max smiled. "Actually, I'm rather flattered. We need to ask you a question. One of our friends has gone missing. She has short grey hair and is wearing a bright orange hooded sweatshirt. We thought she might have come down this path."

Jason smirked. "What's it worth?"

"Jason, shut up," the girl said. "We did see someone like that earlier. She was with a man and another woman."

Max looked at Rita, and then turned back to the girl. "How did she seem?"

The blond shrugged and said, "Fine, I guess. She was laughing."

"Okay, good. Was the man in uniform? A ranger, or maybe a sheriff's deputy?"

"I don't think so."

"What did the other woman look like?" Max asked.

123

Jason pointed at a third boy. "She had hair like Blake." He snorted. "Heck, she looked like Blake."

Max looked at Blake. His hair was close-cropped with bangs—almost an early Beatles look. She tried to picture a woman she knew with hair like that.

Rita stepped forward. "Where did you see them? Which way were they headed?"

Max was surprised, but was glad Rita thought to ask an important question that she had forgotten.

Jason raised his hand and said "Hey!"

"What?" Max asked, a little disgusted with his antics.

"There's some caves in the ravine when you get close to the waterfall." He pointed up the ravine. "I think they were going there." He shrugged his shoulders and waggled his eyebrows.

Max had had enough of Jason. "Young man! This woman could be in danger and we need help to find her and make sure she's okay. Could you get serious for a minute?"

He had the sense to look a little embarrassed. "Sorry. The caves are the only thing in that direction. There aren't any trails at that end, so they would have to climb a pretty steep hill to get out."

"Thank you. That wasn't hard, was it? And that's very helpful." Max turned and started to continue down the hill. The blond girl spoke up again.

"When you come to an old signpost on your left, the caves are above that. They used to have a trail and signs leading up there, but the caves got to be a drug drop."

"I understand. Thanks for that information," She said to Rita. "That's a relief, that someone has seen her, and that she didn't appear to be in distress."

"Who is the man or the woman, do you think?"

"I don't know. " She stepped sideways down the hill a few more feet to the bottom where the walking would be easier. Rita followed and they headed up the ravine in the direction Jason had indicated.

Even though the waterfall trail had been rough and not well maintained, it was a piece of cake compared to the bottom of the ravine. Small boulders had rolled down the hill and required vigilance. Soft spots left by recent rains threatened to swallow up the end of Max's walking stick—or perhaps the whole thing.

"Quicksand," Max said.

"What?" Rita said, looking down at her feet.

Max smiled and waved a hand. "Sorry. I was just thinking when my sisters and I were young, we went to the movies every Friday night, and someone was always falling in quicksand. The Three Stooges, Roy Rogers' horse, Zorro—every major character seemed to run into quicksand. But as an adult, I've never seen any—although this soft ground is pretty close."

Rita chuckled. "You're right. I'd forgotten about that."

125

A few places, Max detoured up the side of the ravine to avoid some really risky-looking spots. Their progress was slow.

"Oh! Rita said suddenly. "Maybe you should call Jessi and tell her what we found out. She gave you her number, didn't she?"

"Good point." Max moved to the side, set her water bottle on a boulder and leaned her walking stick against it. She pulled out her phone and scrolled through the contacts. She looked at Rita in surprise. "I don't know her last name!"

"Just look under 'J', " Rita said with a little smirk. "First names are listed too."

"Oh. Right. This must be it—Jessi Daniels?"

"Yes."

Max punched the number, and let the phone ring several times. Finally it switched to voicemail. "Jessi, this is Maxine Berra, Carole's sister. Rita and I are down in the ravine. We just talked to some kids who said they had seen someone who looked like Babs. She was with a man and they thought they might be headed to the caves below the waterfall trail. Call me when you get this." She hit the off button and said to Rita, "Let's see if we can find that broken sign post."

CHAPTER ELEVEN

RITA TOOK THE LEAD, but the progress wasn't much faster. They could still hear the kids in different parts of the ravine but didn't see any sign of rangers or deputies. Finally Rita halted and pointed to a thicket of wild shrubs with a broken post poking out of the top. "That looks like the old signpost they were talking about. Go ahead. I'll follow."

"Fine. If you see me start to slide, get out of the way!" Max planted her walking stick before each step and grabbed a sturdy-looking branch to pull herself up. It was slow going. She had a feeling Rita was frustrated at the pace, but she couldn't help it.

When she reached a level spot about five feet square, she stopped to catch her breath.

"This was probably a little hasty. I don't know anything about these caves, do you? I thought they would be a little more obvious."

Rita was shaking her head. "No idea."

Max tried to brace herself so she could scan the hillside above them. Sheer walls of rock peeked through trees and shrubs that implausibly grew out of the solid surface.

"I can't see anything," Rita said. The whine was coming back into her voice.

"I never heard anything about these caves until those kids mentioned them."

"Neither did I."

"Well, it looks like the entrances must be small and hidden instead of obvious. I'm surprised I haven't heard back from Jessi." She pulled out her phone. "That's why. One bar. Let's go up a little farther and see what we can see."

They didn't try to talk, and other than a few grunts, some falling rocks, and buzzing flies, the afternoon was quiet. Places that were too steep for a seventy-three-year-old to stand, Max negotiated by dropping down to hands and feet, gorilla style. She was reaching for another branch as a handhold when out of the corner of her eye she caught a glimpse of bright orange behind a bush. She stopped and pointed.

"Look over there—something orange."

Rita said, "I see it!" and clambered sideways to the area. She was able to gingerly stand beside the bush and pulled it back.

"There is an opening here. And it looks like Babs' hoodie but I don't think anyone could fit in this cave."

Max tried to stabilize her position. It was becoming more obvious that this was a very foolish venture. "I think you should leave it there and we should

−" Her phone rang. Gripping the branch tighter, she reached in her pocket, but lost her walking stick and watched it clatter down the hill. Jessi was on the phone. Her message must have gone through.

"A ranger and a deputy sheriff are here to help organize the search. Where are you now?"

Max could feel her left foot slipping. "Somewhere we shouldn't be. There's a path that goes down in the ravine behind the bench where Babs and I were waiting. How about if we meet you at the bottom of the path? We just found Babs' hoodie and we can show you where."

"But where−all right, the bottom of the path behind the bench." She hung up.

"We're going back down. Leave the hoodie so they can see where she was."

Rita looked over at where Max clung to the creaking branch. "I'll go first. Go down on your butt." She demonstrated by lowering herself to the dirt and picking her way down from root to branch. Max followed suit, trying not to think about scrapes on her hands and rips in her clothes. This climb had to be one of the dumbest things she had ever done. By the time they made it back to the bottom, they both had scratches, as well as twigs in their hair.

Max brushed her jeans off. "Well, that wasn't the smartest move. Let's head back to the bottom of that path." They made their way back down the ravine. The kids had moved to the other side of the ravine and were climbing on some other boulders. The blond girl waved.

Max and Rita could see and hear some of the Glampers coming down the path. They were having as much difficulty as Max and Rita had.

Buzzy was the first one down, followed by Jessi and Carole.

"Where were you when I talked to you?" Jessi asked. "It sounded like you were in a hole in the ground or something."

"Worse," Max said, and explained where they had gone. Ranger Mayers was behind Jessi and listened carefully to Max. The kids came down from the rocks and stood a short distance off, watching the Glampers and whispering back and forth. Leah, Brooke, and Lois reached the bottom.

Max motioned the blond girl over. "This is the young woman who told us she spotted Babs," she told Ranger Mayers.

"What's your name, Miss?"

"Berta Robbins."

"Can you tell me what you saw?"

"The woman she asked me about—" Berta indicated Max, " — in an orange hoodie and she had short grey hair—came down that path you just came down. She was with a man and that lady." Berta pointed at Leah.

Leah's mouth dropped open. "What? I haven't seen Babs since we went up to the waterfall."

Buzzy stepped forward. "That's right. Leah's been with us up there the whole time."

Ranger Mayers turned back to Berta. "Are you sure this is the woman you saw?"

Berta looked flustered. "I—I think so. I guess that woman was wearing a different jacket. Maybe she just looked like her—I didn't see her up close. But, she had hair like that."

"Okay. And where did you see them go?"

Berta pointed up the ravine. "That way."

Once again, Jason wasn't to be left out. "We think they were going to the caves."

The ranger nodded. "Thank you for your help." He turned and started up the ravine. Max walked along side him and explained hers and Rita's search. He said, "That area is pretty treacherous. I want you to show me where you climbed up, and I'll take it from there."

"That's fine. I have no desire to go back up there," Max said.

When they reached the broken post, she pointed to the route she and Rita had followed. "I think we saw that hoodie about halfway up, but we left it there so you could see where she must have been."

"Thanks." He started up the hill. The women milled around the area. Leah worked her way over to Max.

"Max, I'm worried." She kept her voice low.

"Well, I think we all are."

"Yes, but I told you I got a text from my sister Tammy that she is in the area."

"Yes, I know."

131

"We look a lot alike."

"You mean—?"

"It could be."

"But does she know Babs?"

Leah shrugged. "I don't know how she would."

Buzzy had come up to them and heard the conversation. She cleared her throat, startling both Leah and Max.

"I might be able to help. Those kids said a man was with them too. Right?"

Max slapped a mosquito on her arm. "Yeah, they did. In fact, I'd forgotten about them mentioning the woman until the girl just told us again."

"I suspect the man is Owen Balzac." Buzzy turned to Leah. "Do you know if your sister has any connection to him?"

"No, I can't imagine that she does."

"Where does she live?" Buzzy asked.

"Over in Potterville, not too far from here."

"I believe Owen and Granger have an office in Potterville."

"I think she works in an insurance office—wait! Maybe it's investments? Is that possible? She hasn't talked to me much since our mother died—I'm not sure what she does," Leah said, rubbing her forehead. "Oh, my God. What has she gotten herself into?"

Max put her arm over Leah's shoulders. "I'm sure it'll be okay. All we know is that the woman with Babs has a haircut similar to yours. That's not damning evidence."

Carole came over. "Max, is Lil still waiting at the bottom of the falls?"

"No, she was tired and I took her back to the camper. She's the one who contacted the rangers."

"Oh, good. I can't believe what is happening here. Do you think Babs will be okay?"

Max shook her head. "I don't know what to think. I can't imagine why she left that bench to wander around down here."

"That's why I think she's with Balzac. She trusts him and would go where he says," Buzzy said.

"True." Max looked around the ravine, suddenly realizing darkness was seeping in. Solid clouds filled the sky above them and obscured the sun. At the bottom of the steep hillside with the thick trees, visibility had definitely declined.

Ranger Mayers returned to the bottom, sliding sideways as much as stepping. He held the hoodie and spoke to Max and Buzzy.

"I didn't find anything other than this, but we have more deputies coming to help in the search. It would be best if you would all return to the campground and wait there for news. We don't want to risk losing or injuring anyone else."

Lois spoke up. "We could help in the search."

He put his hands on his hips and thought a moment. "No offense, but maybe some of you younger ones could help. We will have some volunteers from town, but in this terrain, anyone who has balance

133

problems or difficulty walking needs to keep themselves out of it, okay? Those who are able-bodied to take part, meet up at the bottom of the waterfall path."

There was some grumbling among the Glampers, but Buzzy took charge. "Let's go, ladies! We can talk about what you want to do when we meet up at the end of the path. We've got quite a hill to climb first." She started down the ravine and the rest followed.

Max had dreaded climbing the path back to the bench but found it relatively easy compared to the route she and Rita had followed up to the caves. She stumbled a couple of times. The ranger had likely been referring to people like her when he talked about 'balance problems' or 'difficulty.' After they reached the bench and started back down the path, Carole moved to the side and waited for Max.

"You aren't going to take part in the search, are you?" Her tone indicated she expected an argument and she narrowed her eyes at Max's answer.

"My ankle's still pretty sore and that trip into the ravine didn't help any. But I'm thinking maybe someone should be checking the park buildings and shelters. Along the roads. Places like that. I can drive around and do that."

"Good idea. Okay if I go with you? I think I have a park map in the camper that has all of those buildings marked."

"Sure. I'll talk to the Ranger when we get to the bottom and tell him what our plan is."

"Good idea."

When they reached the bottom, bringing up the end, the ranger and Deputy Bryant had gathered the rest of the women in a group on the narrow point of land overlooking the waterfall pool. Bryant first asked who felt they might have difficulty with the search. Two women Max didn't know raised their hands.

"Thank you for your honesty. Perhaps you can return to the campground and serve as conduits for messages?"

They both nodded and one, a short woman with thin red hair, said "Sure, we can do that. We're in site 32."

"Thank you. And what is your name?" The ranger got out his notepad.

"Diane," said the redhead.

"Mary," replied the other.

"Diane was just diagnosed last month with MS," Carole whispered to Max. "She doesn't like to talk about it, but she's very careful about what she does."

The ranger proceed to divide the other women into teams of three and Deputy Bryant assigned them areas around the ravine and waterfall to search.

The deputy took over the instructions. "As you know, we don't know whether Mrs. Grangersmith is gone of her own free will or not. But because of the incidents in the last two days, we have to take all precautions. If she *has* been taken, her captors could be dangerous, and you must be careful. You will just be looking for signs of where she has gone and *must* contact us immediately if you see anything." He gave them all his phone number.

Each left as they got their assignments. When he got to Max and Carole, Max said, "I'm not able to do the search in the woods either, but we have a suggestion." She described her idea.

He nodded and thought about it a moment. "There will be other searchers and deputies checking other areas of the park, but it wouldn't hurt to have others in cars looking for any sign of these people. As I said, don't take any chances!"

CHAPTER TWELVE

THEY HURRIED UP THE STEPS and back down the campground road. Max started her car while Carole went in the camper to find her park map. She carefully shut the door as she came back out and darted to the passenger seat.

"Lil's asleep," she said as she closed the car door, taking care again not to make too much noise.

"Good. Let's see that map. I'm thinking that the authorities probably have the entrances blocked or at least watched. If Babs is being held by someone, he or she might hide out somewhere inside the park until those roadblocks are removed."

"So one of the park buildings would be a good spot."

Max pointed at the beach house at the north end of the beach. "I noticed that when we were at the campfire the first night."

"Possible. But that's on the other side of the boardwalk going down to the bottom of the waterfall path. They would have had to get Babs past those kids again and under the boardwalk. What about the round barn?"

Max shook her head. "If it's open for tours today, there would be people in there, and if not, it would be locked."

"It's not open today. I heard Buzzy say that's why we were doing the tour yesterday."

"Okay." Max backed out of the campsite. "Let's check out the beach area first. There's a shelter there too but it's wide open." She squealed a little tire as she pulled forward on the road. Leaving the campground, she turned left down the beach road. The overcast sky seemed to be getting denser, making seeing into the understory trees and shrubs more difficult. They parked in the same area that Max had the night of the campfire and she pulled her walking stick from the back seat.

Carole led the way to the structure along the edge of the beach where the transition to woods made the ground a little firmer.

"Doesn't look like it's been used lately," Carole said. A round limestone tower anchored two wings. The main door was locked with a large padlock. Max walked along the right wing looking in the dust-coated windows. Wooden stools were stacked upside down on several dark brown picnic tables; otherwise the room was empty.

"No sign anyone's been here recently."

The walked back to the tower and along the left side. An opening in the left wing had no door. Once they peered inside, they realized there was no roof either.

"Must have been part of the old dressing rooms. A lot of the old ones didn't have roofs. Looks like they made it into a patio area." Carole pointed at a couple of round tables with broken umbrellas. Huge cobwebs draped from the corners of the limestone walls and bird droppings covered the cement floor.

"Not somewhere I'd want to party," Max said. "Obviously, no one's been here. Let's take a quick look around outside before we go."

They hurried around end of the north wing and Max ran into Carole as she stopped short. Pools of backwater greeted them, flooding the trees and stumps.

Carole held up the map. "The lake must be really high. *That* doesn't show on here."

"Another reason why it would have been very hard for them to get to this area. Let's get back to the car. When we get there, call that Deputy Bryant and tell him the beach and beach house are clear. See if anyone else has found anything."

"Right."

Max pulled back onto the beach road and as they drove up the hill to the main road, Carole made the call. When she hung up, she said, "No other sightings and they haven't left the park."

"Not by the road anyway. I imagine there are other ways to get out." Max slapped the steering wheel. "I just remembered, yesterday when we were at the barn, Babs said that Owen Balzac is a volunteer there. That means he might —"

"—have a key!" Carole finished for her.

139

"Yes!" Max sped up a little as she turned on to the main road, slightly over the park speed limit.

Carole leaned forward, peering at the sky. "Looks like we could get some rain." A resounding clap of thunder confirmed her observation.

By the time they rounded the curve and had the barn in sight, streaks of lightning split the sky.

"Do you have a slicker or poncho in here?" Carole asked.

"No. It's in my suitcase."

The visitors' parking lot at the barn was empty. Max pulled in and they jumped out of the car. The temperature had dropped considerably in the last few minutes. As they approached the main entrance, they could see that the doors were padlocked together.

"Let's try the basement," Max said. They pulled their jackets close around them as they bent into the rising wind and edged around to the basement side entrance. Max motioned Carole to duck as they passed each of the windows.

There was no padlock on the basement door, but rather a regular key lock, so they couldn't tell if it was unlocked or not. Max passed the door and edged up to the side of a window. She took a quick look inside.

Carole crouched down beside her. "See anything?"

"No. Too dark." She looked around at the woods and a small parking lot behind the barn. "How would they have gotten here? I don't see a car anywhere."

Carole pointed toward the woods. "It looks like there's something there in those trees."

"Where?"

"Behind that big oak. I can see what looks like the bottom of a tire." She took off toward the tree line, running and stumbling in her crouched position. Max followed but at a slower pace. Hopefully no one was inside and looking out one of the windows. This was about as dumb as climbing that cave hill in the ravine. It began to rain.

Carole reached the oak tree and pulled back some branches. A camouflage tarp covered what looked like a small car or golf cart. Carole pulled a corner up.

"An ATV?" Max said.

"A Gator. Bob was thinking of buying one shortly before his heart attack."

Max turned toward the barn. "Do you suppose the owner is in there?"

"I'll call the deputy."

"I guess you better."

Carole dialed Bryant again. She explained where they were and what they had found. She didn't want to put it on speaker, so held the phone out so Max could hear it.

"We'll be there in a few minutes. Don't try to go in there." He hung up.

"If anyone looks out the front, they'll see the car," Carole said.

"I don't think any windows look out that way. The basement isn't exposed on that side, and there were only a couple of windows on the main level."

"I hope you're right. Should we try to get back to the car?"

"It's raining harder."

Carole chuckled. "I don't think my hair matters much at this point—"

"What was *that*?" Max interrupted.

"What?"

A scream broke through the noise of the rain and thunder. "That!"

"No, I won't!" The voice was shrill and alarmed.

Max started for the barn. "It came from inside."

"We're supposed to wait…"

"Not when someone is screaming! C'mon!"

They didn't try to crouch down or hide in any way. Max felt her ankle give a couple of times. They were both soaked by the time they made it to the side door.

Carole pulled it open and peered inside. The light from the windows was so dim that all they could make out were the stanchions between the tie stalls encircling the center.

"I don't see anyone," Carole whispered.

But they heard a sob. "Sounds like it's coming from the other side," Max said. She started to creep counter clockwise around the outside. They gone about a quarter of the way and just passed the hanging manure bucket, when they heard a noise behind them.

142

"Ladies!" Owen Balzac walked toward them, carrying a mean looking knife. "I thought I heard some interlopers. This wasn't very smart of you."

He herded them a little farther around the circle. "Stop."

Max noticed a movement between the manger and the silo. Babs was seated on the floor leaning against the silo, her hands and feet tied and duct tape over her mouth. Next to her, Leah sat crying. The woman rubbed her eyes with the heels of her hands. No, it wasn't Leah. It must be her sister Tammy.

For want of anything intelligent to say, Max blurted, "What's going on?"

Owen smiled. "I think that's pretty obvious, don't you? And you two are obviously in the way. This complicates things." He kept the knife pointed at them. "Don't try anything stupid. I may not be able to get both of you, but are either of you willing to sacrifice the other?"

Carole gripped Max's elbow.

"Of course, with that fancy car of yours, in a park like this, accidents can happen. And you're old. I'm sure you've lived good lives. You're just way too nosey. Tammy! Bring that duct tape over here and hogtie these gals."

Tammy got up, wiped her eyes again, and stumbled out between the stanchions with a roll of tape in her hands. She seemed to be a reluctant accomplice. She must have been the one screaming. She pulled

143

Carole's arms behind her and wrapped her wrists with several loops of tape.

"Get her mouth," Balzac said. Tammy complied. Balzac kept up a running commentary on how stupid they were, and that he had nothing to lose.

Max thought she heard the door but couldn't see it around the curve. Out of the gloom, a figure appeared. It was Rita. Max's brief glimmer of hope flamed and burned out. In spite of Rita's almost normal behavior in the ravine earlier, she seemed too erratic most of the time to count on now.

Since Balzac was talking and Tammy was busy taping Carole's ankles, neither heard Rita's approach. Suddenly, she threw herself at the hanging manure bucket, jolting it forward along the track and into Owen Balzac's back. The heavy steel bucket threw him forward face down. The knife went skidding across the floor.

"Grab that knife, Rita!" Max yelled and dropped down butt first on Balzac's back. He let out a scream of agony, and she thought with satisfaction that she must have landed on the same spot where the bucket had hit him. Even though she wasn't sure she would be able to get up again.

Carole's eyes were wide, and Tammy stood with her mouth open. "Get that tape off of her!" Max yelled at Tammy. Tammy nodded and began ripping the tape, first from Carole's mouth, then her wrists and ankles.

Carole rubbed her wrists. "Max, are you okay?"

"We all will be when the deputy comes to pick up this turd. Help Tammy get Babs free, would you?"

They heard a siren, and Max said, "Rita, that was awesome! Will you go up and tell the deputy where we are?"

"Sure!" Rita took off at a run.

Balzac began squirming and kicking his legs, yelping with pain at each movement.

"Carole, let Tammy do that and come sit on this jerk's legs!"

Carole returned from the manger area and kneeled on Balzac's legs. Once, freed, Babs hobbled out of the manger area, stiff from being trussed up. She came over and put a foot on one of Balzac's arms.

She was shaking her head. "Carole, you told me your sisters were amateur detectives, but I never envisioned anything like this."

"I know, right? Remind me later to tell you about the time Max drove a snowblower and chased down the bad guy who was driving a sleigh."

"Really? Incredible!" Babs looked more relaxed and comfortable than anytime since Max had met her. She guessed being rescued from a kidnapping might do that.

CHAPTER THIRTEEN

THEY ALL LOOKED UP as they heard the door open. Balzac began to struggle harder. Max slapped him across the back of the head.

Rita's shrill voice bounced off the brick walls. "They're this way. Max is sitting on that guy's head!"

Max said to Owen, "See? It could be worse."

Deputy Bryant came into view, followed by Ranger Mayer and another deputy.

As they got close, Bryant said, "All right. Let him up, ladies." He already had his handcuffs out.

Babs pulled Max to her feet and Rita helped Carole up. Bryant snapped the cuffs on Owen as he asked Babs, "Are you Barbara Grangersmith?"

"Yes, I am."

"Did you come here with this man willingly?"

"No, I did not."

He then noticed Tammy. "And you are…?"

She hung her head. "Tammy Doyle," she muttered.

He examined her more closely. "You look familiar. Have we met before?"

"No." She sighed. "Maybe you met my sister, Leah."

"Ah, yes." He frowned. "What's your part in all of this?"

She started to cry again. "Mr. Balzac is my boss. I run his Potterville office. He said I had to help him teach Mrs. Grangersmith a lesson or I would lose my job. I already lost all my inheritance when Mr. Balzac took the money. I can't lose my job."

"That's a bunch of hooey!" Balzac shouted.

"Be quiet!" He turned to the other deputy. "Take him to the station in your car. I'll deal with her."

"Can we leave?" Max asked. "It's been quite a day and Babs needs to rest, I'm sure."

"I'm going to ask Ranger Mayer to take her to the clinic first to be checked out. We will need statements from all of you, but it can wait until tomorrow morning. You aren't leaving the area before then, are you?"

"No. Tomorrow is fine."

By the time they returned to the campground and filled Lil in on the events, Max was ready to brave another shower. But first she felt it necessary to tell Leah what was going on with her sister.

The rain had quit and Leah was sitting under her awning doing a crossword puzzle. Max explained what had transpired in the round barn.

"What did Tammy say? Why would she do something like that? I mean, I told you she was a little unbalanced, but murder?" She ran her hands through her hair, tugging on it as if pain would help.

"I don't think that she understood his real intentions. She said he wanted her to 'help him teach Babs a lesson.' That could be interpreted a lot of ways."

Leah closed her crossword book and dropped it by her chair. "I need to get to the station and talk to her. She's still my sister. Where's the station, do you know? Wait, Deputy Bryant gave me his card. I'll call him and find out where to go. Oh, God, I'm glad my mother isn't here to see this." She folded her chair and stuffed it under the camper and turned in a circle, confused. "My purse. Where did I put it?"

"Do you want me to go with you?" Max said.

"No, no. You've had enough today. I'll be fine." She went in her camper and came out with her purse on her shoulder, and phone in her hand. She took a deep breath and looked directly at Max. "Thank you for telling me."

"Let me know how it goes."

"I will." She got in her truck and made a phone call, Max assumed to the deputy. She seemed a little calmer as she started the truck and pulled out, giving Max a wave as she left.

Max returned to Carole's campsite to get her shower things.

"I saw her go by," Carole said. "Is she going to see her sister?"

"Yes. She called Bryant before she left and I think he calmed her down some. What a mess. Well, I have to get a shower."

Lil laughed. "Good luck with that. Buzzy said the group has decided to order pizza for supper. Lois will go pick it up. Do you have a preference?"

"Anything but pepperoni."

WHEN SHE RETURNED, Lil said, "How was it? I need to do the same."

Max hung her towel over a low tree branch. "Better. I checked out all the stalls before picking one. The second from the end is pretty good. Stay away from the first one. There's a handicap stall also that you would certainly qualify for."

Lil got up. "I don't need that, but I'm glad you did the research on the others."

"Where's supper going to be?"

"Carole said at Jessi's camper."

AFTER ALL THREE HAD SHOWERED and donned clean clothes, they felt better able to face the world. Carole grabbed a bottle of wine for Lil and herself, and Max mixed a drink in her insulated tumbler. They carried their drinks and their lawn chairs up to hill to Jessi's campsite. Rosie pranced alongside. She seemed to sense there was pizza involved.

The deputy had brought Babs back and Jessi put her in a chaise lounge and told her to stay put. Rosie and

Marilyn, Jessi's Labradoodle, stood guard and willingly accept Babs's strokes and scratches.

Max sat beside her. "Can I get you anything?"

Babs smiled. "No, I'm fine. Jessi's getting me some ice water. I think you've done enough for me today. How are you doing?"

"Better after a shower. What did the clinic say?"

"Just a few scratches and bruises. Nothing serious. I was lucky."

"Have they figured anything out, did he say?"

Babs shook her head. "He'll know more after they question Owen. They hope anyway."

Jessi brought Babs a class of water. "She's staying with me again so I can keep an eye on her. I'm thinking of chaining her wrist to mine." She grinned at Max.

Lois arrived with pizzas, and Sophie and Brooke helped her carry them to a serving table. Max got plates for Babs and herself and returned to her chair.

"How did Owen convince you to leave the bench and go with him?"

Babs shifted a little in her chair. "He and Tammy came by—they had been down in the ravine and were telling me about the caves they found. They wanted to show them to me. I was feeling better and rested, and I trusted Owen completely. He's been so good to me since Grayton went to prison. So I went with them. I left a note on the bench."

Max shook her head. "There wasn't anything there when Rita and I got there."

"I've thought about that, and I suspect Owen picked it up after I started down the hill. I don't understand what he was trying to do."

"I have a theory, but maybe we'll learn more from the deputy tomorrow."

"What is your theory?"

"I'd rather not say until we know more. So how did you get to the barn?"

"We went to the caves and by that time, I was exhausted again. I told Owen I wanted to go back and he said there was an easier way out and then he could give me a ride to the campground. We climbed the hill toward the road—it wasn't really easier. He had one of those ATV things parked along side the road and Tammy drove. Owen sat in the bed behind me."

She drew a breath. "When I could see that we were going away from the campground, I protested and he slapped some duct tape over my mouth and held my arms." Babs shivered with the memories.

Rita arrived, late as usual, grabbed some pizza, and plopped down at the picnic table.

"The hero of the day!" Max said, with a flourish of her hand. "How did you know where we were?"

"Oh." Rita looked a little embarrassed. "Um, I was going to town to pick up a lawn chair at WalMart. I thought there were plenty of people searching. . ." She trailed off and took a bite of her pizza. "Anyway, I saw your car at the barn, and that got me worried."

Max reached over and patted her on the back. "Well, I for one am glad it did. We might not be here. And hitting Balzac with that manure bucket was genius!"

Rita blushed and concentrated on her pizza.

Leah's truck came slowly down the road and pulled into Jessi's parking area. Leah got out and headed for Max. Several Glampers spoke to her, patted her on the back, or gave her a hug. She sat on the end of a picnic bench facing Max.

"You look a little better," Max said. "Did you learn anything from Tammy?"

"Yes—her side of the story anyway." She turned to Babs. "How are you doing, dear?"

"Better. I was just telling Max what happened. What did Tammy say?"

The other Glampers had gathered around, munching on their pizza and listening intently.

"She worked for Owen, as you know, and I found out she had invested all of her inheritance from our mom with Owen."

Babs patted her arm. "Oh, dear, I'm so sorry."

"She says he pretty much blackmailed her into going along with his scheme. He planned to take you back to the woods after dark when the search ended and push you over a cliff. She also thought he planned to knock Max and Carole out and push their car over a cliff."

Max huffed. "He would do *that* to a classic Studebaker? H really is a jerk."

Babs covered her eyes and groaned. "Why was he doing all this?"

Leah grimaced. "Your life insurance would be added to the pot that would be paid out to the litigants."

"I wondered about that," Sophie said.

"But there's good news," Leah continued. "Tammy said that Owen was the one embezzling the money. Your husband knew nothing about it."

Babs sat up. "I *knew* he was innocent. Is she willing to testify to that?"

"Yes. She says—and I believe her—that she had no idea he planned to hurt you. I think she's been scared straight, as they say."

Max straightened. "Wow that's good news for both of you. You know Tammy said in the barn that Mr. Balzac took the money. I thought she was just mixed up."

"So who stole the stuff from you and removed the chocks?" Lois asked Leah.

"Tammy. She kept the chandelier because she knew it was valuable and put the rest in Babs's storage compartment. Owen gave the camper a shove later that night, and he also set the fire."

"What about the other burglaries?" Brooke asked.

"They think that was someone else. Owen and Tammy just took advantage of it to cause confusion."

"He's going to go to prison for a long time," Lil said.

"That's what Dan said," Leah said.

"Who's Dan?" Patrice asked.

153

KAREN MUSSER NORTMAN

Leah blushed. "I mean Deputy Bryant." She smiled. "And by the way, he's very impressed with what this group can do."

Lil gave Max and Carole a knowing look.

Buzzy got up. "Well, who wants more pizza? And I think Diane's got a cake."

The Glampers busied themselves polishing off the pizza and cleaning up while Jessi started a fire and Patrice got out her guitar.

154

Thank You...

For taking your time to share Max and Lil's adventures. Just as the sound of a tree falling in the forest depends on hearers, a book only matters if it has readers. Please consider sharing your thoughts with other readers in a review on Amazon and/or Goodreads. Or email me at karen.musser.nortman@gmail.com.

My website at http://www.karenmussernortman.com provides updates on my books, my blog, and photos of our for-real camping trips. Sign up on my website for my email list and get a free download of *Bats and Bones*.

To my Beta readers, Ginge, Elaine, and Marcia, thank you for all of the great catches and suggestions. And to all of my readers, especially my advance reader team, words are not enough.

The inspiration for the Mystery Sisters was memories of my Great Aunt Mary, who taught phys ed in Missouri until she was in her seventies. She owned a Studebaker and during the summer would drive up to southern Minnesota, pick up my grandmother, and off they'd go to California or Connecticut or some other exotic place (in my teenaged mind). My cousin says they argued constantly, but they made trip after trip. I stole the names of the sisters (but not the personalities) from three of my youngest aunts--the ones who were between my and my parents generation. They were the 'cool' aunts—young and hip. And they were a great example to us all.

OTHER BOOKS BY THE AUTHOR

THE MYSTERY SISTERS

Reunion and Revenge: Maxine Berra and Lillian Garrett, sisters in their seventies, travel together to visit friends and relatives in Max's 1950 red Studebaker with her Irish Setter, Rosie. Does that mean they are amicable companions? Not at all. But when, during a family reunion, the murder of a family friend throws suspicion on their shiftless younger brother, they put their heads together to try to save him.

Foliage and Fatality: Seventy-something sisters, Max and Lil, visit western Pennsylvania, partly to see Lil's son Terry and his family, and partly to enjoy to colorful fall foliage. The sisters volunteer to help staff a fund-raiser haunted house. The house has amazing special effects and a haunted garden. It is hugely popular and should bring in a lot of money for the new school auditorium. What could go wrong?

Double Dutch Death: Sometimes tiptoeing through the tulips can lead to murder! Max and Lil, seventy-something sisters, visit their cousin Bess in the middle of the Tulip Fest. But things don't turn out so rosy for a couple of Bess' acquaintances who end up pushing up daisies.

157

canoeing mishap and a couple of bodies. Frannie tries to stay out of it--really--but what can she do?

The Lady of the Lake: (An IndieBRAG Medallion honoree, 2014 Chanticleer CLUE finalist) A trip down memory lane is fine if you don't stumble on a body. Frannie Shoemaker and her friends camp at Old Dam Trail State Park near one of Donna Nowak's childhood homes. But the present intrudes when a body surfaces. Donna becomes the focus of the investigation and Frannie wonders if the police shouldn't be looking closer at the victim's many enemies. A traveling goddess worshipper, a mystery writer and the Sisters on the Fly add color to the campground.

To Cache a Killer: Geocaching isn't supposed to be about finding dead bodies. But when retiree, Frannie Shoemaker go camping, standard definitions don't apply. A weekend in a beautiful state park in Iowa buzzes with fund-raising events, a search for Ninja turtles, a bevy of suspects, and lots of great food. But are the campers in the wrong place at the wrong time once too often?

The Space Invader: A cozy/thriller mystery! The starry skies over New Mexico, the "Land of Enchantment," may hold secrets of their own. The Shoemakers and the Ferraros, on an extended camping trip, find themselves picking up a souvenir they don't want and taking side trips they didn't plan on.

Real Actors, Not People: Frannie Shoemaker and her friends go camping to get away from the real world. So they are surprised and dismayed to find their wilderness campground the production site of a new 'reality' show--Celebrity Campout. Reality intrudes on their week in the form of accidents, nature, and even murder. They handle the situation with their usual humor, compassion, and mystery solving, because...camping can be murder.

Corpse of Discovery: Over two hundred years ago, famed explorer Meriwether Lewis died on the Natchez Trace under mysterious circumstances. Historians still argue whether it was suicide or murder. That shouldn't affect a weekend campout in present day for Frannie Shoemaker and her friends, but it does. They meet interesting characters at a mountain man rendezvous and get mixed up as usual with the strange goings on. Because camping can be murder!

Mask of Death: During the pandemic, camping was supposed to be a fairly safe activity. That's only if you don't camp with Frannie Shoemaker. Frannie and her husband Larry commit in the fall of 2019 to take on a campground hosting job in the spring of 2020. In that time, the world turned upside down and their job came with a whole new set of challenges. But of course, where Frannie's involved, other trouble can't be far behind!

159

We are NOT Buying a Camper! A prequel to the Frannie Shoemaker Campground Mysteries. Frannie and Larry Shoemaker have busy jobs, two teenagers, and plenty of other demands on their time and sanity. Larry's sister and brother-in-law pester them to try camping for relaxation-- time to sit back, enjoy nature, and catch up on naps. Join Frannie as "RV there yet?" becomes "RV crazy?" and she learns that going back to nature doesn't necessarily mean a simpler life.

A Campy Christmas: A Holiday novella. The Shoemakers and Ferraros plan to spend Christmas in Texas and then take a camping trip through the Southwest. But those plans are stopped cold when they hit a rogue ice storm in Missouri and they end up snowbound in a campground. And that's just the beginning. Includes recipes and winter camping tips.

Happy Camper Tips and Recipes: All of the tips and recipes from the first four Frannie Shoemaker books in one convenient paperback or Kindle version that you can keep in your camping supplies.

THE TIME TRAVEL TRAILER SERIES

The Time Travel Trailer: (An IndieBRAG Medallion honoree, 2015 Chanticleer Paranormal First-in-Category winner) A 1937 vintage camper trailer half hidden in weeds catches Lynne McBriar's eye when she is visiting an elderly friend Ben. Ben eagerly sells it to her and she just as eagerly embarks on a restoration. But after each remodel, sleeping in the trailer lands Lynne and her daughter Dinah in a previous decade—exciting, yet frightening. Glimpses of their home town and ancestors fifty or sixty years earlier is exciting and also offers some clues to the mystery of Ben's lost love. But when Dinah makes a trip on her own, separating herself from her mother by decades, Lynne has never known such fear. It is a trip that may upset the future if Lynne and her estranged husband can't team up to bring their daughter back.

Trailer on the Fly: How many of us have wished at some time or other we could go back in time and change an action or a decision or just take back something that was said? But it is what it is. There is no rewind, reboot, delete key or any other trick to change the past, right?

Lynne McBriar can. She bought a 1937 camper that turned out to be a time portal. And when she meets a young woman who suffers from serious depression over the loss of a close friend ten years earlier, she has the power to do something about it. And there is no reason not to use that power. Right?

Trailer, Get Your Kicks!: Lynne McBriar swore her vintage trailer would stay in a museum where it would be safe from further time travel. But when a museum in Texas wants to borrow it, she determines that she must deliver it herself. Her husband Kurt convinces her to take it along Route 66 for research he is doing. What starts out as a family vacation soon turns deadly, and ends with a romance unworn by time. Travel can be dangerous any time, but when your trip involves the Time Travel Trailer, who knows where (or when) you will end up?

<<<<>>>>

ABOUT THE AUTHOR

Karen Musser Nortman is the author of the Frannie Shoemaker Campground cozy mystery series, including several IndieBRAG Medallion honorees. After previous incarnations as a secondary social studies teacher (22 years) and a test developer (18 years), she returned to her childhood dream of writing a novel.

Karen and her husband Butch originally tent camped when their children were young and switched to a travel trailer when sleeping on the ground lost its romantic adventure. They took frequent weekend jaunts with friends to parks in Iowa and surrounding states, plus occasional longer trips. Entertainment on these trips has ranged from geocaching and hiking/biking to barbecue contests, balloon fests, and buck skinners' rendezvous. Out of these trips came the Frannie Shoemaker Campground Mysteries and now The Time Travel Trailer Series.

After the loss of her husband, Karen now drives a small motorhome named Agatha after the Queen of Mysteries.

Sign up for Karen's email list at www.karenmussernortman.com and receive a free ereader download of *Bats and Bones*.

Manufactured by Amazon.ca
Acheson, AB